Sarah —
Everyone
an evil hero
in them ;

CUPID

JADE EBY

KENYA WRIGHT

Jade Eby

Copyright © 2015, Jade Eby & Kenya Wright

Cover Design by Jackie Sheats

Interior Formatting by Jade Eby, www.jadeeby.com/services

All rights reserved. This eBook is licensed for the personal enjoyment of the original purchaser only. This eBook may not be resold or given away to other people. If you would like to share this book with another person, please purchase an additional copy for each recipient. If you are reading this eBook and did not purchase it, or it was not purchased for your use only, then please purchase your own copy. Thank you for respecting the hard work of this author. The characters and events portrayed in this book are a work of fiction or are used fictitiously. Any similarity to real persons, living or dead, is coincidental and not intended by the author.

JADE EBY

KENYA WRIGHT

This is dedicated to our brains. You gave us all the creativity, ideas and fortitude to pull together this badass story.

CHAPTER ONE

CUPID

There was a man in the darkness, and that man held a bloody bow and arrow.

The bow was carbon, barely three pounds, and with a leather grip. Long ago, he'd carved ten lines into the handle.

Each mark represented his kill, and tonight, he would add two more lines.

Blood always came, when the man drew back his bow. The arrows were fast and easy to pull, and oh how he loved to make them fly.

He loved to watch the blood drip down a graying corpse, inch by inch, staining flesh and radiating the scent of death.

He loved to watch that crimson liquid pool around dead bodies,
his targets,
men who'd hurt women for sport,
fathers that raped children,
husbands that cheated on loyal wives,

and
brothers that stole the innocence from their sisters. He loved to watch them die.

And when they did, he crouched down, hummed his mother's lullaby, sniffed the rotting air, and peered into their lids, to see their mortality glaze over vacant eyes.

That night, the bow and arrow had done everything it had been brought to the rich man's condo to do. Mr. Neil Carson, millionaire extraordinaire, lay dead on the kitchen floor. His mistress's corpse was sprawled along the granite counter with her bare bottom up, red bra hanging around her tiny neck, and her head resting in the sink. Water dripped from the faucet, wetting her hair and filling the space with a haunting rhythm.

"This was too fast." The killer frowned. "Too easy."

Blood dripped from his fingers, spilled red dots onto his polished shoes, and stained the front of his tuxedo shirt. He would have to change before returning back to his mansion. No doubt he'd scratched his hair due to his restlessness, and got blood on his blonde waves.

At least I can wash this mousse stuff out of my hair.

Usually he wore his strands in disarray, only getting a haircut the few times he had to show his face at a board meeting in his corporation or a news spotlight for some innovative food product his staff had designed.

Earlier tonight, his mother obsessed over his hair, called her stylist, and had his head done up in ridiculous waves.

She'd had him on her eighteenth birthday. A monster had

gotten her pregnant. But that hadn't stopped her from loving Asher the minute he came into the world. In fact, there was no person, no man who could possess the love she had for her son.

"Oh darling! You look fabulous!" His mother embraced him right as he stepped out of the hallway.

"I look ridiculous." He patted down his tuxedo. "I won't wear this thing all night."

His mother laughed. "Asher, you'll wear it or I'll give you hell." She slid her hands down his muscular arms as if marveling at his strength.

Asher had been working out more, testing his speed in the morning during runs, timing the instances he scaled up walls or dashed down a hall without making any sound. He'd been getting better, just for the sake of never getting caught.

He always had to be two steps ahead of everyone—the police, his victims, and the few curious rich folk, who put down their caviar and took notice of all the wealthy men dying around them.

Asher's mother stopped her hand at his wrists, turned it over, inspected him, and then glared. "Do you have to wear those cufflinks?"

He glanced at them. They were classic steel and oval shaped. On the surface, diamonds outlined skulls. "I like them."

"They're ruining the effect."

"I disagree. The skulls add to the effect." Nodding at a maid who hurried past him, Asher traveled down the hall and

toward the spiral staircase.

The stairs were one of the main reasons he'd bought the mansion. Several film production companies had made them famous and shot numerous scenes from the top view. Gangsters in mafia movies fell to their death from that level, their legs and arms wagging as they plunged to their descent. In the few romantic flicks done in his mansion, lovers raced down those stairs—the hero hoped to catch the woman he might've lost, the heroine rushed away, yearning to finally be done with the broken cycle. Directors had documented those spiraling steps, noting the artistry in the carvings on the rail. Tiny angels decorated the inside, where most people placed their hands as they traveled down. Horned-demons covered the outside.

Asher relished in the demon etchings, pleasured in the wicked grooves that pressed against his fingertips each time he rushed up or took his time going down.

They were eye candy. When he stood at the top and gazed below. A wild rose of stairs greeted his eyes—this sort of spiraling down of petals made from iron and cream marble.

Tonight, those stairs also served as Asher's escape from his mother.

"Where are you going?" She trailed behind him. "I haven't smelled you yet?"

"What?" He scrunched his face up in horror.

"Smelled." She rushed after him. "I haven't smelled you yet."

"Goodnight, Mother."

"Asher!"

He stopped at the top of the stairs, checked his watch, and hoped he'd have time to go over preparations for this evening. His gloves, other equipment, as well as his bow and arrows needed to be near his motorcycle that was parked on the far south of his grounds, at the end of a massive garden.

His mother inhaled him.

Shaking his head, he smirked.. "Do I smell good?"

"What are you wearing?"

"Soap and water."

"No cologne?"

"Good evening, Mother." He continued down the stairs.

"Where are you going?"

"The party will begin in two hours. I'm sure you want to go over everything with the kitchen staff."

She paused, looked down at her flowery robe, touched the curlers in her hair, and turned around, rushing back to her bedroom at the end of the hall. "I should get dressed."

He grinned. "You look beautiful just the way you are."

"Oh stop it!" She glanced over her shoulder, right before entering her room. "By the way, you look amazing this evening. You look like Jay Gatsby himself, right from the novel obsessing over his beautiful debutant Daisy Buchanan. I've invited many women this evening for your event. There should be tons of Daisies there."

"Great." He shook his head.

"Don't you roll those beautiful blue eyes at me," she huffed. "Remember. Mother knows best."

"She does?"

"Yes, Asher."

"Sometimes you scare me," he muttered under his breath and hurried down the stairs.

The killer pushed the memory out of his mind and returned to his predicament. Boredom. The only reason he'd been okay with having the party at his mansion this evening was that it provided him an alibi to kill Neil Carson and his mistress.

Now I'll have to go back. It's like eating a bad meal that was huge, yet unsatisfying. I don't even feel like I've ate. I'm still hungry. Do I have time to feed myself some more? No. That's not the way. I have to be careful, have to plan my kills, not rush into them. But. . .do I have time for one more?

Due to living on Ovid Island, he never truly had time to himself. The area was named after the famous poet Ovid, and catered to the most affluent people in Miami.

The island was south of the city's coastline. Residences were exclusive. One needed a boat to get there, and even then, security checked for written approval and identification before the person could step onto land. For that reason, no one really left the island. Instead, they remained there, partying on their estates and getting into everyone's business.

Beyond Ovid Island's bustling business district and the breath-taking blue rippled waves - there were rich men and women hiding secrets. No one asked questions. No one wanted the truth.

Even Asher didn't leave the island to kill. Along with the

boredom, he'd gotten lazy, swimming in the dullness of day-to-day life among the affluent.

I don't have the time. I should go.

Hundreds of guests would still be in Asher's mansion, partying well into the morning. They'd expect him to show his face after the fireworks exploded in the sky above his grounds, and all wished each other a happy new year.

Not that his alibi wasn't secure.

News cameras filmed his New Year's Eve speech an hour ago. His staff kept all glasses topped with expensive champagne. Some of the men and women were probably so drunk in that moment, tomorrow there would be made-up stories of him and his exploits all over the party.

He gritted his teeth and stared at the corpse in the center of the room. "I didn't even get a chance to hear Neil beg."

Silence filled the space.

He flexed his bloody fingers and gazed at the dark figure on the floor, cloaked in shadows and decay. All the excitement of the evening fled from his chest. That hollowness returned, that empty feeling he always felt as he walked around day-to-day—running his corporations, escorting movie stars, and smiling for the flashing lights that followed him everywhere.

Not a good New Year's Eve at all.

He exhaled. There was nothing else to do in the kitchen, but leave.

That night, he would go home, drink, smoke, fuck a sexy stranger, and do all of the things that normal people did.

Yet in his head,
a blackness would unfurl,
spiraling down into him,
just like that huge staircase in his house,
the one that looked like a black and white rose,
but on some days,
stared back at him like an evil eye.

 A gloom would spark in the center of his core and rise up to meet that dwindling blackness.

The hunger would return,
strengthen,
and yank away at his senses.
He would be enraged with blood lust,
similar to a thousand year old vampire that just crawled out of the grave,
after centuries of a deep sleep,
and in need of some young maiden's ivory neck.

 The killer licked his lips at the thought. In his mind, he saw a young woman, in one of those old gowns with elegant fabric, hooped skirts that dripped with silk, and a stiff corset top that held her bosom up on display. He could see the lovely maiden with spiraled hair, bobbling as she raced away in a foggy forest, the vampire right on her feet.
 "No," she would scream.
 But the vampire would not care.

The hunger was too strong.

He would capture her in his arms, slip his fingers along the curve of her neck, push his fangs out of his gums, and pierce the beautiful flesh.

"Neil!" a woman yelled in the condo and shoved the killer out of his daydream. "Neil!"

Who the hell is that? No one was supposed to be here tonight.

And then the kitchen door opened.

He froze.

A woman's voice filled the air as she yelled out the dead man's name again, "Neil?"

The word came out like a melody as if she'd intended to sing Neil's name, and changed her mind, once it left her lips. "Neil?"

Who is this?

"Neil?" Her voice drummed through to the killer's bones.

He bit his bottom lip and squinted to get a better look of her. It was too dark, too black and hard to see.

No one else was supposed to be in the condo tonight. Not Neil's wife, personal assistant, and even his staff. Who is this? Wife or someone else?

Inhaling the air, Asher blended back into shadows. His heart battered against his chest. Plans had changed. The urge to kill more itched in his gums and sparked in his fingers as he tightened his grip on the bow.

Yet, did she deserve to die?

No. Not by my hands, at least. Who knows what she's

done to another? Women can be evil little creatures. Mother taught me that.

"Neil?" The woman appeared in the opened doorway. Light glowed around her. She was a black woman. That much he could tell. He couldn't make out the features of her face nor the color of her eyes or the fullness of those lips as she called Neil's name again. Long, wavy black hair hung past her shoulders. He couldn't see much else, yet her silhouette kept his attention.

Neil, you lucky bastard. Who is she? This can't be your wife.

Asher's research on the man had been lackluster. Instead of taking weeks to follow him around, he decided to kill Neil based solely on island gossip. Everyone had called him an emotionally abusive man-whore, yet when they spoke of his wife, they did it with respect in a sort of sadness, like they felt bad for the poor women would been shackled to the beast.

I should've at least broken in a few times while he was home with his wife. Like I did with the others. Watched them sleep. Checked out their hidden secrets.

"Neil?"

Is this his wife or another mistress?

"Neil?" The woman had a lush frame—curves and softness. Part of him craved a closer view. The rest of him tensed in fear of being caught.

If she spotted him, then she would die.

There would be no question in his mind, if the moment

came, he would draw back his bow and hit the target on her chest in seconds. Sometimes, he let a few women go, if he deemed them innocent. Tonight, he didn't have the time to judge her.

Turn around. Leave.

Unease crept up his spine.

"Never leave witnesses behind." His mother would always say as she held him close to her bosom, rocked his small body, and sung that lullaby over and over. "Kill them all. It's only us in this world. No one else needs our protection."

The kitchen door squeaked as the woman pushed it open wider.

What made her call Neil's name over and over, and stay there peering at the shadowed kitchen? Did she feel something? Was she not scared or nervous? Did she sense the terror around her?

Death pricked at the average person's skin, whether they knew it lingered around them or not. It was hard to ignore. She should've sensed the morbid situation around her, and been forced to back away.

"Neil?" she said into the darkness, but didn't enter the kitchen. "Neil, are you in here? I don't feel like any of your games tonight. If you're hiding and plan on jumping out at me, as usual, then you're in for a very violent surprise."

She placed her hand on the wall next to the door way, slid it up and down, flipped the switch, and gasped when the light didn't turn on.

This is when you run.

She froze right there, not moving her finger or the rest of her body another inch. Thoughts must've spiraled around in her mind.

What are you thinking? There's no light in here, yet the rest of the condo's lights work. Tonight is not the time to investigate. Tonight is when you turn around and leave. Tonight you escape a destiny that wasn't meant for you.

She stood there, silent. Besides the dripping from the faucet, quiet continued. A sweet perfume traveled into the room and journeyed to the killer.

What scent is that? Vanilla or something flowery? Roses. It must be roses.

Hiding in the shadows, he gripped his loaded bow and inhaled her fragrance some more.

Turn around, sweet one. Tonight is not your day to die.

She cleared her throat and stepped inside. "Neil? I'm serious. You told me to meet you in the kitchen, but. . ."

So Neil had asked his wife or whatever to come to the kitchen? Why would he do that when he was having sex with his mistress? Had he hoped she walked in? This must be why others gossiped about him being a manipulative douche.

She inched in further. "I swear on everything. I don't have time for more of your fucking mental games."

Turn around.

From the shadows and with smooth precision, the killer pointed the arrow at her chest. If she took one more step inside the kitchen, he'd release the wire and let the arrow glide through the air. Knots built in his gut.

Turn around, sweet one.

A sigh left her lips. "I'm done playing your games, Neil." She ran her fingers through her hair and stepped back. "You couldn't even give me tonight. Could you? What's the point of being your wife, if I see you less than all of your mistresses, and get absolutely no respect!"

Interesting.

The kitchen door slammed behind her.

Asher leaned forward and patiently listened for the sounds of her departure—footsteps pounding away, keys jingling, doors creaking open and shutting back.

Don't worry, sweet one. Neil's gone. You won't need to play those mental games with him anymore.

Minutes passed. She made a few more noises here and there in the apartment, yelling out his name from time to time. Another few minutes went by.

Finally, the condo's front door slammed, and Asher guessed that the sweet-scented woman had left and he was finally alone.

He returned his attention to the dead man on the floor and crouched low to get a good look at the corpse in the darkness.

Pulling out his tiny flashlight and turning it on, he studied Neil's face. "You had a beautiful wife. What made you decide to have her come to the kitchen tonight, while you knew, you would be fucking your mistress from behind? Was your wife supposed to see that? Did you think it would be funny?"

Asher winked at the corpse. "Now who do you think will

be laughing, once tomorrow's morning news reports your dead body found with your slutty secretary in a secret apartment that was paid for illegally by your company's investors? Poor Neil."

Asher inhaled the space. A harsh odor radiated from the stiff's flesh.
There was no other fragrance that left a bigger imprint in most people's minds.
When one smelled death,
there was no way of getting it out of their head.
It sat,
that scent,
in the crevices of the brain where gloom clung to cells and veins,
and where nightmares were birthed,
and horror fulfilled.
Yet, he inhaled it all.
To him,
death mingled with childhood memories,
nightmares soothed,
and taking one's life released the tension from his shoulders.
Blood warmed the coldness in his chest,
just for a few seconds,
before his core returned back to an empty cave made of ice.
What was her name?

He walked over to the dead mistress's naked body that

was slumped over the counter. Asher thought back to the moment, right before he surprised the evil pair. Neil's pants sat at his ankles as he barreled his pecker into his mistress.

"Let's make her cry," the mistress had groaned. *"Show her how you make me scream your name."*

At first, Asher wondered who the mistress had been talking about. Who had she wanted to make cry? For that reasoning alone, he didn't give her the chance to escape. Making people cry wasn't really nice after all. She got an arrow in her back, and then Asher gave all of his attention to Neil's shaking frame as he pissed on himself, right in the kitchen.

"Let's make her cry."

"Now it all makes sense." He grabbed the arrow sticking out of Neil's chest and yanked it away. "You wanted to hurt your wife for whatever reason. Maybe it got you off, added to the orgasm. Fucking another was no longer enough. Now you needed the games."

Asher wiped the arrow's tip on his pants. Blood smeared on the material. He'd planned to burn everything he wore once he got to the back of his grounds.

"I get it, Neil. Boredom makes us do wicked things." He rose and headed over to the mistress. "Too bad your wife couldn't have seen me kill you. Would she have liked it? She smelled so good. A woman that smells like that would use logic. Mother always said, a female that could master all of a man's senses around her, is one that's using the maximum power of her brain."

Laughter fled his lips. He pulled the arrow out of the mistress's back and wiped it off.

Okay, Asher. You've had your fun.

But for whatever reason, he didn't rush away like all the other times he'd killed. For some crazy reason, he remained there, breathing in everything.

Soon, he'd have to sneak out of the condo, jump on his motorcycle, speed through traffic, and enter the back of his mansion, hide his tools, clean himself, and rush off to party until dawn.

Soon, he'd have to dive into meaningless conversations with faceless people whose names always blurred together, with the intoxication of the wine, and the artificial feminine giggling that lingered afterward.

Soon, he'd have to shift from killer to Asher Bishop, heir to the Bishop multi-millionaire food empire.

Soon.

Releasing a long breath, he stared to the rich man's corpse for a few more seconds, but that time, he didn't sing his mother's lullaby, as he did with all the others.

That time, he stood over the dead body and thought of the fragrance of roses.

CHAPTER TWO

DIANA

Diana didn't know why she was still married to Neil. She was no longer young, naive and under the illusion that real love existed.

Neil was a man with eclectic tastes—mostly in women.

But being the good wife on his arm fueled her to stay. To pretend. They looked good together. His mother loved her and she was the darling of any party they attended. Diana stayed because she had no real reason to leave.

The truth though, was that she was tired.

Restless.

Desiring something more than what Neil had given her.

She wanted something otherworldly, if there were such a thing. Some kind of experience or love or drug to take her to new heights. Or maybe she was just stuck reporting the same shit news day in and day out, while fucking the same man night after night.

She was due for a change.

As she climbed the three flights of stairs to their lush new condo, Diana thought maybe Neil had something exciting planned for them. He'd texted her a cryptic message about meeting him in the kitchen, but when she arrived, she was met with silence and darkness.

She called out his name, "Neil?"

No response.

"Neil?" she said again.

The door to the kitchen was cracked an inch and as she pushed it open, something strange fell over her. Like all the air in the room was being sucked up and pressing against her flesh.

It was cold, too.

Much colder than it should have been, given Neil liked to keep the thermostat set firmly at sixty-eight degrees.

Shivering, she reached for the light. When it didn't turn on as she expected, the feeling in her bones grew heavy. As if she was on the precipice of discovering something horrible.

She shrugged it off. This was just another one of Neil's jokes. Something he thought was funny, though Diana had long ago lost her patience with his brand of funny.

She sighed into the darkness, disappointed in herself.

She'd let herself believe that there was a chance of...what?

A steamy shower fuck?

Rose petals scattered on the counter? A glass of champagne ready to be drank?

No. That's not what this was at all.

Those fantasies flowed out of her as easily as she conjured it up.

"Neil?" Diana backed out of the kitchen, her veins thrumming with electricity.

Why had all the lights worked in the rest of the apartment, but not in the kitchen?

Why had she felt as if she'd stepped into an incubator of energy instead of her pristine condo?

There were things Diana knew weren't meant to be questioned, but that never stopped her before. She was a goddamn reporter for shit's sake and she'd lived and would eventually die from finding out the answers that no one else bothered to look for.

Sometimes investigating fulfilled her.

Sometimes it ruined her life,

like with her dad.

At ten, she'd discovered a body in her back yard.

That dirty space behind her house had always been her favorite place to dig around. People dropped quarters there. She found other treasures too—a pretty earring, a wrinkled page from porn magazine, and two turquoise rocks that glinted under the sun.

That day, she'd dug and shoveled like any other afternoon—break the soil, lift it up, sling it to the side, and repeat.

Yet, an odd energy filled the air. It buzzed around, all electric and hot as fire.

Things changed even more at the appearance of a graying hand right in the area where she shoveled. Unmoving fingers sat in the ground. Stiff and pale. The whole hand was embedded in the backyard's soil and standing up like a flower. And even worse, three copper rings covered three fingers, just like her babysitter Gabby's hand.

"*Gabby?*" *Diana whispered.*

A normal girl would have jumped up and screamed.

A normal girl probably wouldn't have been shoveling in the back yard in the first place.

But, Diana kept digging,

searching,

and pushing away the dirt.

More of the dead body appeared. It caused terror to jump inside of Diana's rib cage. She found it hard to breath, yet she dug some more, that intense, electric sensation sparkling along her skin.

"*Gabby.*" *Her fingers shook as she stopped the shoveling and peered forward.*

Diana's babysitter, Gabby had pink hair. That day, those colorful strands didn't shine bright and appear so cool. Dirt clumped to knots and on some parts of Gabby's head, worms slithered along maggot-infested grooves along her opened skull. Violent, purple lines circled Gabby's neck like an extravagant necklace. The dead girl only wore a red bra and panties with one high-heeled shoe half-way off of her right foot.

"*Gabby.*" *Diana's bottom lip quivered.* "*What happened?*"

The babysitter gave Diana no answer, as she'd done many

times before, always providing Diana with funny, nonsensical answers that seemed to test the laws of reality.

"I'm so sorry, Gabby," Diana whispered.

Gabby's eyes stared up at the sky and mirrored the cloudy image in front of them.

In no time, Diana rushed into the house, bypassed her parents, and called the police.

Her mother and father had been arguing that morning anyway. They'd been doing that a lot lately. Fighting about her dad's lack of work. She paid them no mind and focused on helping Gabby.

Perhaps, Diana should've stopped them and explained what she found, before calling the police. Maybe things would've turned out different for them all.

But she didn't do things like normal children.

Diana had been the one to find the dead body, so she'd been the one to call the police.

And through tear-blurred eyes, she'd been the one to watch her father get arrested for Gabby's murder. She'd been the one to hold her mother as she fell to the ground and cried.

One thing Diana had not realized was that a dead young white girl in a poor, black man's yard, didn't trigger court-approved justice in the eyes of society.

Her father died that night in jail. No one knew who sliced his neck. A week later, the police found Gabby's actual killer three houses down from hers.

Back in her husband Neil's extra apartment, she remained frozen in the kitchen's doorway.

Something is different. It's that same feeling like before. Why?

Just like when discovering Gabby's body that same electric sensation prickled at her skin. Diana couldn't figure out what to do next, part of her urged to investigate, the rest screamed to race away.

Is Neil okay or is this one of his games? I bet he's in here. Watching me as I stand here, shaking. He's probably naked and stroking himself.

She thought back to all of Neil's many games—inviting women to their table on date night and outrageously flirting with them, emailing her videos of his sexual exploits, intentionally screaming out other women's names right before he came inside of her, and the worst of all, telling her how much he loved her, declaring how much he cared, and then laughing out loud and denying it all with disgust.

With Neil it was a constant struggle to stay within reality. He was a question she was always trying to decode. One of the many demons on her back that she'd earned for accidentally killing her father.

"Neil?" she asked in the darkness.

Neil had become more predictable with age and marriage, yet there were still secrets he locked up tight enough to keep Diana curious. His kitchen message was certainly enough to make her wonder about his intentions.

> **Neil:** Come to my apartment on Dickens Road. I want to show you something.
> **Diana:** What is it?

Neil: I want to show you how much I care about you. Come to the kitchen.

Diana: It's New Year's Eve. We should be out celebrating.

Neil: Stop arguing. Just come.

Diana: You better not be messing with me.

Neil: Hurry. I can't wait to show you what I have planned.

Diana sighed.

Maybe he wanted to feel the same thrill as Diana did? Did he concoct a series of elaborate clues that would end in a romantic candle-lit dinner?

Probably not. That isn't Neil's style, and why am I feeling that same electric feeling?

Gabby's frail, cold body flashed in her mind. All her nightmares, no matter how different or complex, always ended with that image of Gabby's corpse.

Cold chills ran up Diana's spine.

"I'm done playing your games, Neil," she said, just in case he was there in the kitchen.

She ran her fingers through her hair and stepped back. "You couldn't even give me tonight. Could you? What's the point of being your wife, if I see you less than all of your mistresses, and get absolutely no respect?"

Diana slammed the front door on the way out of the condo. She would check their other condo first before heading to her newspaper's office. Although she didn't need the job's money, she craved all of the other things that came with it—the clicking of keyboard keys as she typed away her findings on something she'd exhausted days in research on, her co-workers conversation that stimulated her mind and sometimes shook the walls deep within her heart, and just the plain old freedom of being away from Neil's evil games.

I guess I'm spending New Year's Eve in the office, like last year.

Her office never disappointed her as Neil did. It never told her lies. Never expected things from her that she didn't want to give. It never drug her down so low that she found it difficult to crawl to safety.

Besides the night is still young, and I have plenty of work that needs to be done before Gregory returns from his vacation in Cancun and starts hammering away questions on my article deadlines.

If Neil wasn't going to make an effort to keep her around, well then he would find out just how much fun she could have without him. Diana was determined to take back what she'd lost in her marriage with Neil.

Adventure, excitement, and herself.

The latter was the most important. Somehow she'd lost the things that made her, Diana. Neil's harsh games had chipped away at her very soul. At times she blinked her eyes, and yearned for an escape, unsure of the view that lay right in front of her.

She knew she should've left Neil long ago, knew it deep down within her core.

Still, she stayed.

Maybe, that's my New Year's resolution. Get away from

Neil.

As she pulled out of the parking spot below the condo, she swore she saw something pass by the kitchen window. The shadow of a figure creeping away, someone tall and holding something on their back.

See. I knew you were in the apartment, Neil. What were you going to do if I came all the way into the kitchen?

"Go fuck yourself, Neil." Blinking, she shook her head and put her foot on the brake. No other images went by any of the windows in the apartment, which was strange.

Wait a minute. Did I really see something or not? You know what? Who cares?

She sped off.

The time had finally come—Neil had driven her crazy enough to lose her mind. Shadow people and all. He was going to be sorry when she finally found him. She would make damn sure of that.

Diana's office was more a home than either of her condos.

She lived, breathed and slept in the place she was passionate about. Ink and paper and stale coffee engulfed her senses, but she craved it like a junkie does a fix. She'd never tire of the smells and atmosphere of a newsroom. Of keyboard clacks underneath her fingertips. Not even the piles of papers scattered around the floor bothered her.

She did it because it was in her blood.

Reporting.

Hunting down the truth.

She was no longer that little girl that made a huge mistake that cost her father his life.

Things had changed.

Someone could try to hide from Diana Carson, but they never got far.

She found them.

Always.

Literary awards stacked her shelves at home. They awarded Diana for her addiction to curiosity, her constant yearning to know it all.

At one am, Diana sat with the Mirabelli file in her lap. She'd gone to the other condo, and as expected, Neil was nowhere to be found. She called his cell phone only to get his voicemail. She left him a nasty message and went straight to the office.

Have fun playing your games by yourself.

She'd much rather be with the case file of a murdered man than sitting at home alone with a bottle of wine.

At least she could be productive at the office.

At least she could pretend there wasn't a part of her that throbbed with pain at all the things Neil had done to her. She could pretend to be strong, independent and victorious.

She forced herself back to the file in her hands.

Jackson Mirabell, the charming, crack-addicted son of Richard Mirabelli the second who was the creator and CEO of Mirabelli Technologies. Diana had met Jackson at a party once. He was just like every other man who came from wealthy inheritances. Arrogant, attractive as hell with a shit ton of addictions he mostly kept well hidden.

Is that what got him killed?

She couldn't decide which was the ultimate cause, his penchant for expensive white powder in clear baggies or his affliction for hurting the hookers he hired. Either way, Jackson had been found two days ago in his first floor apartment, a hole in his chest, blood dripping out the sides of his puckered lips.

The hole.

It was a point of contention between the police and the medical examiner. Not a bullet hole. Too large. No one could explain it and Diana was perplexed as to how Jackson Mirabelli really died.

The concierge told police he went up to his room with a petite blonde in stilettos, but she never came back down. Police found no sign of the woman. Either the concierge was lying or this girl simply… disappeared. Diana's best guess was that the woman got a lucky break, escaped when she could, before things got bad.

I have to figure out who she is, and talk to her. I bet one of the madams on the island would know who she was. Someone will point me in the right direction, whether they know it or not. I have to find out why the girl never came back down and her body wasn't found. She has to be a live, right?

At least, that was what Diana intended to find out. And when she did, she'd be able to piece everything else together.

Who was Jackson Mirabelli in trouble with? How did he get that gaping hole in his chest? And more importantly—how did this girl manage to get away from it all?

Diana glanced at her watch and realized two whole hours had passed. It was almost three in the morning and she still hadn't heard from Neil.

Tingles shook through her. Neil wasn't a good husband, but he was attached to his phone as if it were a synthetic limb. He would have called back by now.

Something is wrong.

CHAPTER THREE

CUPID

"Asher! You are a fool!" His mother snatched the Ovid Island newspaper from his hands and threw it to the ground. "Fool!"

"Good morning, Mother." Asher didn't even try to pick the paper up. Instead, he leaned back in his chair and returned to his breakfast.

The chef peeked her head in and looked at him. That day, her thick braids were pulled up in a ponytail that showed off her lovely chocolate skin.

"Sir, is everything okay?" the chef asked.

"Yes, Grace," Asher said. "We're fine."

"Tell her to go!" His mother paced back and forth, back and forth. "We need to talk, and right now!"

"Calm down and eat, please." He gestured to the table. "Grace made a lovely assortment of goodies today. The eggs are sunny side up, bacon crisp, croissants flaky and buttery."

"You like *your* eggs sunny side up. *I* like them scrambled." His mother passed by Grace and stomped over to her side of the table. "And the damn woman has forgot to set my place again." His mother hit the empty surface in front of where she always sat and frowned. "More and more she forgets to set my place at the table. We need to replace her."

Asher gazed awkwardly at Grace and shifted in his chair. "We're not replacing anyone."

Grace widened her eyes and opened her mouth, but no words came out.

"Grace, don't listen to my mother." He shook his head. "Please, just make her a place."

"With proper eggs," Mother interrupted.

"Sir?" Grace asked.

"I'm sorry. Mother wants the eggs scrambled." He leaned down and picked up the newspaper.

"You want me to make a place for your mother?" Grace asked.

"See! She's an imbecile!" His mother covered her face. "All night I had to repeat myself. Still, she didn't follow any of my orders. None of the dishes presented were from the menu I gave her. Who does this?"

"Mother!" He hit the table hard, which startled both women. Water shook in his glass.

"Is everything okay, sir?" Grace asked.

His mother imitated the chef in a whiny voice, "Is everything okay, sir? Can she not hear us arguing about her lack of ability to do her job?"

"Mother, let's move on." Asher did his best to calm her down. "The party has already happened. Let's just get through breakfast this morning. Grace, please make *proper eggs* for Mother as usual."

"Okay, sir." Grace nodded and turned around.

"And Grace," Asher added.

"Yes, sir." She glanced over her shoulder.

"I don't know what occurred between you and my mother last night, but that is never to happen again. And could you please apologize to my mother?"

Grace looked around the room, not seeing anyone else, but Asher. These moments tended to be the hardest part of her job. She always had to make sure she turned to whatever direction Asher was talking to his dead mother, and then try to address her.

Grace turned to the empty space at the table, years ago, where his mother would sit for all of her meals. "Mrs. Bishop, I'm so sorry about last night."

Asher checked with his mother. "Is that better?"

The old woman crossed her arms over her chest and pouted. "Fine. Now tell her to leave. I can't deal with Grace today, and do you know why?"

"Why?" Asher sighed.

"Because my son is a fool."

Asher forced himself not to roll his eyes. "Thank you, Grace."

Grace nodded, rushed back into the kitchen, and hoped that she could guess the right dish the ghost would love to eat this morning. Half the time it was luck. Other times she guessed wrong and got a stern look from Mr. Bishop. Yet, she stayed with him for all these years because he paid three times as much as most did for a private chef, mainly due to the confidentiality agreement his lawyer made her sign.

The other reason. . . she felt bad for him. After all, he was only hurting himself. What was left of his poor mother now sat in a private gravesite in Miami.

Meanwhile, in the dining area, Asher Bishop argued with his mother.

"And why am I a fool?" he asked.

"There's a dead man in the newspaper this morning." His mother pointed to the newspaper.

"There are always dead men in the newspaper."

"Not ones that you're responsible for."

Asher raised a blonde eyebrow. "Are you sure about that?"

"Well, apparently, you go off now on your own and do whatever you want. So no, I'm not sure about that. Since when do you kill without my approval?" She held her hands in the air and let them fall to her sides. "No matter how many times I tell you to be careful, think things through, and stop your. . .activities. You keep going."

Asher folded the newspaper up and placed it next to him. "The paper said Neil was found with his mistress. All of the stations are focusing more on the scandal, then who actually did it."

"Oh really?" His mother pointed to the paper. "Read some

more."

"I was reading until you rudely took it out of my hand." She frowned and refused to look away.

"Fine. I'll read some more." For the rest of the breakfast, he checked out the front-page story that continued on page nine and took up the whole section in the back. The detail of the arrow wound had been concealed, which meant that the police probably had connected Neil's death to the other men he'd killed last year.

"If you are going to murder again, at least use a knife or gun," his mother suggested.

Asher noticed Grace walking back in with his mother's plate.

"Quiet, please," Asher said.

"Me, sir?" Grace asked.

"No, I'm talking to Mother."

"Okay." Grace offered him a weak smile, held the plate, and looked around the table. "And Mrs. Bishop, where would you like to eat your food?"

"Right where I'm sitting," she snapped.

Grace stared at Asher as if pleading with him for something.

He shrugged.

Maybe, she's afraid of Mother. Most are.

"Umm." He stood up and grabbed the plate. "Thank you so much, Grace. I'll take it over to her."

Grace's face brightened. "Oh thank you so much! Not many people that I've worked for with your status would get up and serve the plate."

"Well, I wasn't always rich. I'm not one from money." Asher winked at her and took his Mother her breakfast. "Mother and I have been very lucky."

"I see." Grace checked the table and took away his empty bowl where he'd been munching on fresh strawberries and yogurt.

"Yes, Mother married very well. . .a few times." He sat back down.

Sighing, his mother picked up her fork. "Why you must converse with these people as if they're on our level, boggles me. These eggs look runny."

"The eggs look fine." He forced a smile.

Grace stared at the untouched plate in front of the empty seat. "Does she not like the eggs, sir?"

"Mother doesn't really like *anything* this morning." He took a sip of his orange juice. "You're excused, Grace."

"Thank you, sir."

Asher returned to the paper. Although the details on the front seemed like the normal things—mystery behind the murder, dim-witted speculation, and broad details. The continuance of the story caught his attention. Out of no where, the news article shifted into an editorial commentary, and Asher didn't at all like the reporter's observations.

Asher reread the passage again.

. . .there is something going on in Auden City, something that we, the citizens of this area, are blind

to. This is the third affluent man that has been found on the island and mysteriously killed.

Thomas Nickelson, owner of Lenwood Oil, was discovered by his wife with a gaping hole in his chest. His head was also face down at the foot of his daughter's bed. His daughter claimed to not see anything that happened that evening due to being asleep.

Jackson Mirabelli, son of leading entrepreneur Richard Mirabelli was found two days ago in his first floor apartment with a similar hole in his chest. The concierge told police that he'd arrived with a woman. However, the identity of that woman still has not been discovered.

Although, the police have not confirmed if Neil Carson died with a hole in his chest, any logical citizen can surmise that if the wound is similar to the other two murdered, wealthy men, then Ovid Island has a serial killer among us.

Asher stiffened in his chair. "Interesting."

"You're getting lazy." His mother pushed her plate away as if she didn't see anything on there that she'd enjoy eating. "You're leaving the bodies out in the open now. You've never done that before."

"It's more fun that way." He grabbed a strawberry from

his bowl and plopped it in his mouth. "I like to let the people in their lives know what they've done."

"Or do you want everyone to know what *you've* done?"

"Meaning?"

"You want some notoriety for ridding the world of scum."

"You're wrong." He flipped the page around to check out the name of the reporter who wrote the article. "Very interesting, indeed."

"What?"

"Diane Carson wrote the article. If I remember correctly, that's Neil's wife. I hadn't realized she was a reporter."

"Didn't you do your investigation before the kill?"

"I previewed Neil's history, but—"

"Fool!" His mother hit the table.

"I needed one more kill before the end of the year."

"You killed the druggie guy three days ago. Was that not enough?"

"His name was Jackson and yes. . .that wasn't a fulfilling hunt." He pulled out his phone and did a search of Diane Carson.

In a few seconds, her picture came up on his screen. The fragrance of roses seemed to radiate from the phone.

That's her. It has to be.

Like he guessed, she was a black woman with a lush color of skin, more rich earth than copper. Her skin looked soft. Asher's fingers itched to touch it. In the picture, long black hair ran past her shoulders.

He scanned through more results for a full body picture. A

few came up. She'd been photographed with Neil at a few charity events. No matter what dress or gown she wore, those lush curves peaked out under expensive fabric.

"Why are you staring at your phone like that?" His mother interrupted his search.

"I'm wondering what type of woman does a news article on her dead husband hours after he'd been discovered murdered."

"Maybe she's crazy."

"Or obsessed," he muttered.

"Obsessed with what?"

"The story. The mystery of it all."

"That's not very romantic. She's in shock, probably keeping busy to get over her husband's death. That's what some new widows do, we all mourn differently."

"That's not what you did when your three husbands died."

She'd really been married four times, but neither Asher nor her, counted the monster.

"No. I didn't mourn by keeping myself busy. I mourned in style." She beamed for this was her most favorite topic of all. "I simply got dressed, wore that lovely black veil—"

"Yes, the one from Tiffany's."

"Oh I'm so mad that you burned it. What a lovely veil."

Burned it? I never did that.

The image of his mother on fire hit him for a moment. He shook his head and that horrific sight left.

His mother laughed. "Each time my husbands died, remember, we would have a big breakfast, just you and I?"

"Yes." He nodded. Sadness slipped over his heart. Suddenly, he didn't want to sit and eat with his mother anymore. He got up as she continued to talk as if he was no longer there.

"Oh you loved those huge chocolate waffles with all of that whip cream. Oh my boy and his sweets. You would do anything for them."

"And I did," he sighed. "I did plenty for those chocolate waffles on those mornings."

"Yes, you did, my lovely little boy." She gestured around them, pointing at the crystal chandelier hanging above them and the huge table adorned in china plates and elegant silverware. "Together we made sure we would never have to work again. You saved us."

Inside of Asher's chest, a storm brewed. A gloom untangled and wound around over and over as if a tornado was threatening to uncoil within a down pour.

"I'll see you later, Mother."

"Busy day?"

"Yes." He kept his back to her, not wanting to deal with his mother, the memories of the husbands, or even that odd flash of her on fire. "I'm going somewhere."

"Can I come?"

He paused and then thought better of it. "No."

"What are your plans?" she asked.

"I have a reporter to meet."

"Tell me you're not serious."

He didn't even turn around as he smiled. "You know what

reporter I'm going to talk to."

"Please, for the love of God, say it is not Diana Carson."

"Who else would I be meeting?"

"Fool!" His mother called after him, right as he rushed up the stairs.

CHAPTER FOUR

DIANA

Ovid Island's police headquarters sat in a turquoise and pink castle with glittery sea shells outlining the roof and windows. Old man Libbey, the longest living resident on the island, had donated the small castle to the force. Due to him being such a power guy in the community, the police chief couldn't refuse.

And so all official police business happened within the candy-colored space. Most newcomers mistakenly thought the police building was a children's museum or art center. Others joked that the facility's décor was fitting because the police represented the biggest jokes on the island.

Most considered them clowns.

Many found them useless.

A few island residents voted to change their turquoise and white uniforms to ones more representative of their true occupations—big red clown purple, squeaky red noses, polka dot parachute pants, glowing suspenders, and flowers tucked in their shirt pockets that squirted out water.

What could these men really do anyway? The police, themselves, barely made enough to pay their mortgage and fund their boat commutes back and forth from their homes in Miami to their jobs on the island. They held no real authority against the rich. Half the time they argued with the residents' lawyers about what they could and could not investigate.

Smart Ovid cops had a plan. They saw the island as a vacation from the mean, dirty streets of Miami where prostitutes strolled, parents abused children, and men shot down each other just for several feet of block space to sell drugs. The clever police took bribes from the residents, kept their pockets heavy, mouths closed, and eyes blind.

The dumb cops sought justice. They peered where others said to turn away. They combed the island, hoping to maintain harmony among the madness that came with people with too much money and time. The dumb ones usually were transferred to somewhere else within months.

As Diana sat in the police interrogation room, she wondered which cop Officer Slattery was, smart or stupid. Could he be trusted or did he have his hand in someone else's pocket, was he another's puppet?

Why am I here? Is Neil in jail? Is that why he hasn't been answering my calls?

The officer plopped down in the seat in front of her, his belling jiggling a little with the movement. The shirt stretched tight over him. Five more pounds and he'd need a new uniform shirt. Another drop of ketchup and whatever else was on the front of his top, and he'd need to go home and change.

"Here you go, Mrs. Carson." Officer Slattery placed a cup of coffee down in front of Diana.

"Why am I here?"

"I just want you to be comfortable before I—"

"Just tell me what's going on. Where's Neil?"

"Well, you see Mrs. Carson. I have. . ."

"Just tell me," she said with more force than she intended.

The officer rested his hands on the table between them and knitted his fingers together. "The condo building's maid, a Mrs. Garcia, discovered your husband's body this morning in the kitchen."

Shocked, Diana didn't even grab the cup or look at it. "Neil is dead?"

"Yes, Mrs. Carson."

"Do you know who did this?" she asked.

"I was wondering if you had any information." He wouldn't look at her. The officer glanced at the wall behind her, the cup of coffee in front of her, and even his fumbling fingers as he twisted them around his watch.

"You're nervous," she said. "Why?"

"I have some more news, and I'm afraid I'm not comfortable with giving it to you."

"You might as well go ahead." She hugged herself and tried to prepare her heart for more.

"Mr. Carson was found in the kitchen with a woman that the maid had identified as his secretary."

Diana slumped back in her chair and rubbed her face with

both of her hands. She hadn't even put on any makeup or changed when she rushed to the police station to see why they'd called her to come.

"Are you okay, Mrs. Carson?" Officer Slattery asked.

"My husband was found dead in the kitchen with his secretary at six in the morning?"

A red tint shaded his face. "Yes."

"Is there something else?" Diana asked.

"I. . ."

"What? Were they found in a compromising position?" she sighed.

"Umm. . ."

"Listen. My husband cheating on me is not news to my ears. Granted, his death is news. His blatant adultery and disrespect of our marriage is what I like to call Regular Tuesdays. You don't even want to know what he does on hump days." An erratic giggle fled her lips as Diana's fingers shook. She grabbed her cup and attempted to calm herself enough so that she could pick it up. "He has something disgusting for each day of the week. Was it just his secretary?"

The officer's eyes widened. "Ma'm?"

She gave up on grabbing the coffee. "Sorry."

"No. I understand."

Do you?

She was supposed to be heartbroken, devastated that her handsome, wealthy, all-American husband was murdered with none other than his slutty mistress.

She had a few tears to shed. They would just happen to be for all the blood that stained the granite countertops and seeped into the marbling stone floor. For all the mess she was left with because of Neil.

Diana wasn't a particularly sentimental woman, but neither was she cold and unfeeling. What it came down to, simply, was that she was so done with Neil and his antics. His sleeping around and acting like she didn't know about it. His righteous, holier-than-thou attitude about everything. His degrading views that Diana should be a trophy wife instead of a whip-smart reporter.

His need to break her down mentally every day with his games.

The Neil she fell in love with—whatever version of love it had been—was not the same man who died with his pants around his ankles.

She had respected him, once. He'd been a formidable man once upon a time, who possessed substance, a man that made her panties wet the minute he flashed his dimpled smile.

That time had long passed.

Yes, Diana Carson was a bit upset that her husband and his secretary whore had been murdered. But, she would get over it rather quickly.

And then, one couldn't forget about Neil's texts to her before he died.

Neil: *I want to show you how much I care about you. Come to the kitchen.*

Diana: *It's New Year's Eve. Give me one day where you're not cruel, please.*

Neil: *I've never been cruel to you. Just come.*

But his intention had been cruel. Neil must've hoped Diana would walk in on him banging his secretary right there in the kitchen.

What did you think would come out of that? Were you going to stuff that whore with your cock while pointing and laughing at me? Or did you think we were going to be in a threesome? You're lucky this murderer found you and her together, before I did, Neil. You might've gotten worse than an arrow in your chest.

Officer Slattery coughed into his hand. "Would you like some tissue, just in case you need to cry?"

"No." She gritted her teeth. "I won't need anything to wipe tears."

"If you need some time to digest this bad news, I could go and give you a few minutes or so to—"

She waved him away. "Go ahead with your questions."

The officer stared at her for a few seconds, perhaps studying the rage that glittered along her eyes.

She must've been an anomaly to the officer because Diana had not slipped into the little, meek widow that most saw on TV shows and movies. Tragedy and death humbled most people. For Diana, it toughened her. Once she heard that her husband had died with his mistress, investigation mode set in. Dozens of questions whipped through her brain.

Who did this? Why? Am I in danger? Was it something to

do with his mistress or was it all about Neil?

"Okay." Officer Slattery tapped the plastic glass behind him, and signaled for someone else to come in. "Captain Rothschild will be joining me as I ask you a few questions."

"That's fine."

Captain Rothschild walked in, and represented Officer Slattery's complete opposite—tall, skinny, and an ironed uniform with no food stains on the shirt. Where the officer could've acted in an automobile insurance commercial about bad luck accidents, the captain could've been rising out of ocean waves and stepping onto a sandy beach as water streamed down his abs.

I bet Rothschild takes bribes. He's too tanned and happy. Meanwhile Slattery looks like he stays up all night, eating at his desk and combing over evidence of unsolved cases. According to Ovid Island, Rothschild is the smart one. Slattery is the dumb one.

Diana focused on Slattery and placed her hands on the table. Her fingers still shivered, but she paid them no mind. To her, she exuded a beacon of strength. Inside, things broke apart and other emotions solidified.

"Go right ahead, Officer," she said. "Besides, I have a few questions of my own."

Both men exchanged nervous glances and then proceeded with their interview. It took all of ten minutes to figure out that Diana not only had an alibi in the form of her condo lobby camera, but that Neil's murder was familiar to the other wealthy and dead men found with holes in their chest. Of course, given that Diana knew she did not murder Neil and his mistress, she was insanely curious as to who did.

Could it have been the same person that killed Jackson Mirabelli?

Diana needed to know the answers.

This guy that I've already been searching for, has now come to me. Why did you kill Neil? Did he have some connection to Jackson, Thomas, or any of the others?

"Did your husband know the other victims well?" Slattery asked, while Rothschild checked his phone. He'd been staring into that tiny device most of the interrogation.

I bet Rothschild is going over Facebook updates or probably taking a selfie.

"Mrs. Carson?" Slattery said.

"Yes."

"Did your husband know any of the other victims?"

"No," she said. "I mean as much as anyone on the island knows each other. It's pretty hard not to remember the name of faces that you see day to day, but did Neil actually spend time with any of these men? No. Not even a golf or game day. Neil spent time with women. All of his employees were females. All of his friends were women he'd known for years. The only thing a person with a penis could do for Neil was either lift something heavy, or point him in the direction of a vagina."

Right at the mention of vagina, she shut her mouth.

Perhaps, I'm not okay. Maybe, I'm just a little bit angry at that bastard.

"Sorry," she blurted out.

"I understand." Officer Slattery glanced over at Rothschild who continued to tap things into his phone. "Okay, so you said you had questions for us."

"Are you certain that Neil died the same way the other men did?" she asked.

"That's not something I can tell you," Slattery said.

"My husband and I have not only contributed mass sums of money to this department, we've also managed to unite with a lot of powerful friends on the island." Diana didn't like to strong-arm cops, but sometimes moments like these called for it. "I don't expect you to tell me intricate details of all the murders, but I do want to know if Neil is being considered as one of the victims of this serial killer on the island."

"Hey," Captain Rothschild held his hand up, but didn't look away from the phone. "No one is saying this is a serial killer."

"He's murdered three men that are similar—rich and white. Clearly, there's someone upset about something and on a mission. This screams serial killer."

Rothschild targeted her with a piercing gaze. "This is not a serial killer." He rose from his seat and headed to the door. "In fact, our questions are over. Slattery, please finish this and make sure Mrs. Carson is taken care of."

The fat officer nodded.

Diana waited for Captain Rothschild to leave, and then attacked Slattery with a look that scared most. "Come on. Tell me something."

"I...can't."

"You look like you work hard." She gestured to his wrinkled shirt. "You spent the night at the station right?"

He nodded.

"All that hard work, and no one cares." She shook her head. "Nothing gets done. No one goes to jail, and if they do, they're out within fifteen minutes thanks to their huge law team. You're tired of it. Aren't you? The bullshit. The evil that breeds from money. The crime that gets ignored."

Slattery formed his lips into a straight line.

"I'm a news reporter."

"I know who you are," he said.

"I always have a wealth of information. It's sad to say, but I could get clues and facts from places on this island that you could never even venture into. I have developed a lot of contacts with many people. I could help you with not only this investigation, but future ones. Additionally, I could get your supervisors off your back at times, just by waving around my money." She smiled at him and offered her hand. "Hello, Officer Slattery. Would you like to be my friend?"

He stared at the hand and didn't shake it. "I've found that friends on this island tend to change into enemies at the most inopportune times."

"Then let's call this a friendly probationary period."

He glanced around as if someone was hiding in the room, and then shook her hand. "What do you want to know?"

"How similar was my husband's death to the other victims?" she asked.

"Just like the others," Slattery muttered. "Hole was the same size, too. Definitely, some sort of hunting arrow. The murderer probably uses a high-tech bow. Something a hunter would use to take down big game."

Slattery, glanced at Diana briefly. "We're going to have to keep this quiet. Don't want to alarm the public. We need to find this guy. And fast."

She shifted uncomfortably in the plastic chair, writhing with the desire to be loose. "Could you get me some copies of the case files for the other murders and any similar ones in the past year?"

Slattery rubbed a worried groove into his chin. "I don't think that's a good idea or that it will do any good."

"You don't have any witnesses."

"This is true."

"I could get you witnesses."

Slattery glanced over his shoulder again. "I. . .I don't want any connection to—"

"Of course not. I would never tell anybody my sources."

Slattery and Diana talked some more. They did so in whispers and nervous checks of the glass window where Captain Rothschild paced and watched them. They shared a few details between each other, and then promised to figure out an appropriate time that afternoon to exchange the files.

Thirty minutes later, Diana was excused, and a female officer had her signing paperwork and answering a few more tedious questions about Neil.

She answered like a robot, yet on the inside,

determination beat within her heart. Unlike other wives who'd just found out that their husbands were brutally murdered, Diana hoped to drown in this mystery, to investigate the people, places, and things the police so often missed. And what would be better than to look into her own husband's death?

Does he even deserve justice? No, Diana. Stop that. Neil is dead. I can't be mad at him.

Yet, anger and sadness bubbled in her chest. She pushed it all aside, blinked the tears away, and considered all the new facts that she'd heard tonight.

I need to find witnesses. That's what the police have been unable to do. I'll need to find the blonde chick that was seen walking in with Jackson. That will be where I'll start. Then maybe I can talk to Thomas's daughter. He was the man found dead at his daughter's head board while she slept. Why would the killer murder Thomas in his daughter's room?

Diana had been in the game long enough to know what she was and wasn't supposed to do. She thought about the news headline she would write later today. It flashed over and over again until it burned into her skull.

A Serial Killer Among Us.

Ovid Island City Police Department would be furious with the article. Her boss would scold her, and then give her his classic wink, but one thing would remain despite it all:

The truth would be out.

He, *whoever he was*, would know that Diana Carson was not the reporter you wanted to fuck with. And if you're going to kill her husband and his pathetic mistress, you are bound and determined to get caught.

So she waited in the interrogation room, as the police tripped over their own shoes and twiddled their thumbs with evidence.

She waited for them to double check her alibi.

She waited for them to notify her that she could not enter Neil's extra sex-fest apartment, due to it being a crime scene.

And she waited and waited some more, the whole time, writing her entire news article in her head, until finally, Captain Rothschild let her leave.

"Sorry about your loss, Mrs. Carson," he said to her as she passed him in the hallway.

"I'm not." She tossed back her hair and let the heavy police doors slam shut on the way out.

CHAPTER FIVE

DIANA

The rest of the day, Diana dived into the murders. She consumed the files Officer Slattery had given her, called up some of her trusty contacts, and was sure she had some good leads to search out in a few hours.

Then a knock came at her office door.

She looked up from her big desk.

A gorgeous man greeted her eyes and said in a deep voice, "Are you Diana Carson?"

Diana was certain he asked a question, though it sounded more like a command. As if the words barreled out of him and fed right into her veins. He was tall, blonde, impeccably dressed in a fitted navy striped suit.

Banker? CEO?

She cleared her throat. "Yes, I am."

He nodded and pulled a chair up to her desk. "I'd like to offer you a deal."

Diana's eyebrows rose.

This should be good. If it involves any sort of sexual bargaining, I'm in.

"Oh yeah?" She took her hand off her mouse and placed it in her lap. "And what's that?"

"I would like you to investigate something for me."

"I'm a new reporter, not an investigator."

He curved those lovely lips into a smirk. "I'm well aware of who you are."

"Then you know that if I'm investigating it, then it's to publish a story. I don't keep secrets. I share them with the world."

"Like I said." His smirk widened. "I'm well aware of who you are. Besides, I believe you would be invested in this deal."

"Why?"

"Because it involves your husband and his. . .horrific demise."

A shudder of sadness ran through her. The reaction disgusted her. Wasn't she supposed to be happy Neil had gone that way? If he'd been a better man, wouldn't he still be alive? Why the hell could she not be okay with just hearing that Neil was gone?

Pushing all of the emotional chaos out of her head, she swallowed and carefully said, "Maybe you should explain what the deal is."

"Are you confident that the murderer you wrote about this morning, is a serial killer?"

She leaned back in her chair. "Yes. Why?"

"Most serial killers have specific victims that they target."

"Yes, this is correct," she agreed. "I think it's at least safe to assume that this serial killer targets rich men."

"Maybe even only rich, white men." He held his hands out as if to say that he, himself fit that category.

"So my article scared you?"

"It freaked out a lot of people."

Diana crossed her legs under her desk. "So back to your deal."

"I researched you."

"Why?"

"Why not? The point is, I looked up your past works." He raised his hands and then clapped them slowly. "You've accomplished great things, Mrs. Carson. In your years as a lowly reporter for the Miami Times, two serial killers were caught due to your investigative reports. You then transferred to the New York Times and cracked a few federal cases on Wall Street. I can go on and on—"

"But there's no need to, I know exactly everything I've done. What is the deal, Mr. . .? What did you say your name was?"

"I didn't."

"Maybe, you should."

"Perhaps, when the appropriate time for personal conversation is over dinner."

"I asked for your name, not your social security card."

"And I asked you out, and you didn't respond."

"I've just been newly widowed."

"So you're single."

"Umm. . .Excuse me?"

"Back to the deal."

"Wait." She held her hand in front of her. "What is your name?"

"Mrs. Carson, I'll tell you my name, after we've agreed to the deal, the one that you will say yes to, because you simply can't say no. I understand this about you, this woman who has justice and curiosity burning through her veins." He raised one finger. "This is why I came to your office, among other things. The first reason was to fund your passion, get you on this supposed serial killer haunting our island and targeting people that look just like me."

She touched her chest. "You want me to investigate this possible serial killer?"

"Yes, and then I want you to give me your number and commit to dinner tonight."

"Okay. No to dinner. Now, back to—"

"I came to see you. To listen to your voice. To inhale your scent. To maybe get a sense of the feel of your skin. And although, this is a bit much coming from a stranger who's just trampled into your life barely hours after your dead husband —"

"Excuse me?" Diana rose from her desk. "This is too much."

"And doesn't it feel good?"

"What?"

This man that sat before her was a tongue twister of sorts.

Somehow he'd lassoed her mind, and had Diana spinning all over the place.

"Doesn't it feel good to have something be too much in your life," he said. "Doesn't it feel good to finally feel something vibrate through to your bones, after this boring and staggered life as a trophy wife for a heartless man?"

"You don't know me."

"I want to." His response exuded confidence that had energy tingling at Diana's toes. "But first, I need your help."

"Finding this serial killer?"

"Yes, and I want to fund the entire manhunt. I'm willing to pay for any resources you need. I'm intrigued. I'm wondering if you can really catch this man, after finding so many others."

"You want me to go on a manhunt?"

"Yes."

"I don't think so."

"Interesting," he said.

"Why?"

"Because we both know you're going after this man. You've probably already started running down clues and witnesses. So why aren't you telling me yes?"

Something doesn't feel right. He's good-looking which explains the bloated ego, but he's also pretty smart, and really good at leaning others toward his way. I can see it in the smirk on his face. He knows I would do this for him. But why would he want it done? What am I missing?

Diana had already decided to trigger a manhunt herself,

but it was personal, something that she needed to solely control. This man's funding would bring up too much accountability and possibly reveal some of her illegal exploits in digging through clues. But even worse, getting into a deal with this guy might not be a good idea, although she couldn't pinpoint why.

"Detective work is not exactly my job," she said, trying to buy herself more time to think about the deal. "I've found criminals, and helped put many to jail, but I also lost even more, and wasted hundreds of hours on investigations that revealed nothing."

"You're a reporter, Mrs. Carson. Of course it's your job. What I'm offering is a once in a lifetime opportunity. I'll fund you however you desire, as long as you at least try to catch the killer. I would even get this worked out with your boss, make this your main story. I have just recently bought a large part of stock with this newspaper. In a way, you could call me your boss too."

Diana's heart thwacked against her chest. "Why would you buy up stock in this newspaper?"

"Why not?"

"Because it doesn't explain your sudden interest in Ovid Island Newspaper."

"It's a grand paper." He shrugged.

"It's a small time set-up that doesn't provide half of the things that USA Today reports, which is why residents still have all the others delivered to their doorsteps."

"I read this paper every morning."

"Why did you buy the stock?"

"I like to own things." He focused his gaze on Diana's face. Those eyes, golden brown with flecks of dancing emerald and sapphire, stared straight into hers. She wanted to look away, but couldn't. They claimed her, right then. He could have done whatever he wanted with her, and Diana would have been putty in his hands.

"You won't own me, whether you have all the stock or even if I agree to your deal. There's no way to own me."

"Interesting." He rubbed his hands together and rose from his chair. "I'm a simple man. I don't try to take much, although I could. These murders interest me, for nothing more than to save my own life. I believe that you could help the police on this island, who basically," he chuckled, "Are just a bunch of buffoons."

Diana didn't believe most of what he said. Sure, he may have been interested in finding the killer's identity just as Diana was. But that wasn't the reason he went out of his way to ask her, and even try to buy up the company. There was something else going on in the background. He was invested way more than he cared to say.

Is he protecting someone or something? Men on this island are always committing treachery in all types of ways. What is the benefit to him, if I find the killer?

"Are you over there considering my offer, Mrs. Carson?" A blonde tendril fell over his eye. He pushed it back and crossed his big arms over his chest.

What does he do for a living? Some sort of fitness thing or maybe body building?

"I'm considering it," she said.

"Just say yes to my deal, and yes to dinner." He unloosened his arms and checked his watch. "I've got to run over to the gym today, so I can be ready for our date tonight."

"You sure you don't want to take a day off from the gym." She looked him up and down, and could care less if he noticed. He'd walked into her office and knocked her off balance. Maybe a bit of flirting would shove him over too. He seemed like a man who needed to be in charge, craved the ability to hunt, what if he was the one that was being hunted?

"You definitely keep in shape. Very sexy."

He quirked his eyebrows. "This is why I know you'll say yes for dinner tonight."

She rolled her eyes. "Because of your body?"

"No, you'll say yes, due to my stamina. I could show you."

"Show me what?" She bit her lip.

He licked his lips and gestured toward her desk. "Show you my stamina."

It shouldn't have happened, but it did. Images cluttered her head. Hot ones, where sweat dripped down his bare chest as he lifted her naked body up, propped Diana on the desk, and rammed into her all night long.

She gasped.

My husband just died, there's a serial killer on the loose, and all I can do right now is think about this man stripping me down and fucking me.

"And now this part of the conversation must end." She walked around her desk and made a show of guiding him out.

"I want my answers."

"I'm giving them to you, as you leave." She opened the door.

He refused to take another step.

"I'll say yes to the investigation, but it needs to be in writing with a budget and all guidelines for legal responsibilities. I'll have my lawyer look over it before signing."

He stepped her way, and got close to her, too close. Barely two inches or so ran between them. The haunting scent of his cologne snared her, made Diana tilt a little forward in his direction and sniff.

God, he smells good.

"Dinner?"

"I'm now a widow." She leaned away from him, and tried to get together her composure. "I don't think it's appropriate to date while mourning."

"Mourning is about healing. Most use wine, food, and other things to help them get through the process. I'll be providing all of those tonight."

"The wine and food?"

He seared her with his gaze. "And the other things."

Speechless, Diana decided she didn't care what his motives were, somewhere under all his lies, had to be the truth. The one she'd figured out. She hoped it was something that ended with the two of them in a luxurious bed together.

She just couldn't rule anything out.

"Okay," she whispered. "But, just dinner."

"Marvelous," he whispered and closed in one of the inches between them. "Tonight at seven pm?"

Backing away, Diana reached for the water bottle on her desk and realized too late that it was empty. She was suddenly parched, her mouth dry and scratchy. She'd never been caught this off guard before.

"Where will dinner be?" she asked."And I don't even know your name. This is ridiculous."

"Asher Bishop." He extended his hand out. The minute his calloused fingers graced Diana's impossibly smooth palm, she felt it again. The same chilling, air-sucking aura that pressed against her from last night, when she'd stood in the kitchen. *How strange.*

"As in Asher Bishop, millionaire and heir to the Bishop Food Empire?"

His smile didn't waver. Not even a twitch. "I see you've heard of me."

Diana's mind worked on overdrive, trying to piece together any other facts she'd heard about the man.

"Dinner at The Cove tonight, then." He interrupted her brain scramble. "I'll have my pilot pick you up."

"Pilot?"

"How else would you get there?" He laughed and Diana's chest was an earthquake. Her bones rattled, her ribs shook and the blood that ran through her veins turned molten. She didn't know what *this* was, but she wanted to feel it again and again and again.

"I've never been to The Cove," she muttered the words under her breath.

But he'd caught them, and frowned. "Shame on Neil for never taking you. You will love it. This a place where men dine with their women, ones that they love, ones that they're hoping to show the whole world too."

"And why are *you* taking me?"

Chuckling to himself, he said nothing else, and walked out without event looking back.

Not one glance over his shoulder or utterance of a smart remark.

He left her there with jumbled emotions and thoughts spiraling in her mind as well as this all-encompassing tremor moving through her limbs.

She wasn't sure what to be more worried about: the fact that Asher Bishop, handsome and wealthy millionaire had just offered to fund her very own murder investigation that dealt with her husband, or that he looked at her with an intensity that set her heart ablaze.

This is all in my mind. Neil just died. I've gotten almost no sleep. I'm probably just a mental mess. What am I even thinking.

Yet, for the first time that day, fear pounded in her heart, and it had nothing to do with the serial killer that had been wreaking havoc on the island. Maybe, it was the deal, and the oddness of the invitation. Perhaps, it was his suspicious involvement or how he'd basically offered her money and his cock all in one swift conversation.

Diana didn't have a hold on too much of what was going on.

All she knew was that Asher Bishop would be her undoing.

Chapter Six

CUPID

"Mrs. Carson has been picked up. We've arrived at The Cove rooftop's landing platform," Asher's pilot said into his phone. "I escorted her onto the elevator. She is now heading your way and will arrive within one minute."

"Thank you." Asher placed his cell into his back pocket, stood on the restaurant's balcony, and stared at the breathtaking view in front of him.

The Cove was a restaurant that sat inside a small bay, sheltered from regular people. Only the affluent dined there, and one could only get to it by yacht or helicopter due to the narrow, restricted water entrance that lay miles outside of Miami.

Time to have fun.

From the balcony, he gazed at Ovid Island far off in the distance.

The poet Ovid, himself, would have been inspired by the

view and written even more poems about abandoned heroines and absent lovers.

Moonlight painted the ocean's rippling surface in sharp, white lines that seemed to cut into its watery flesh. Stars buttoned to the sky and sparkled. A romantic perfume filled the air, something haunting like Diana's scent—roses and ocean.

He inhaled and considered the smell.

I'm being crazy. Her scent can't already be here. She hasn't appeared yet.

After meeting her, face-to-face, those lips and that scent had passed in his mind a few times. It did odd things to his body, made him want to shut his eyes for a few seconds and relish in the daydream.

But it was just for fun, something wicked to do in-between business meetings and his mother's angry rants that afternoon. Nothing more would come with Mrs. Carson. And he believed the little daydreaming about her was completely normal.

Everything is under control. Diana will be nothing more than my avatar in the months to come.

It didn't matter that she'd intrigued him--her skin smoothed like warm chocolate, her beautiful eyes had welcomed Asher into her office and made him want to stand in front of her longer than he'd planned, and that voice. . .it had rocked his core. Those words left her full lips and had rapidly beat inside of him like a damaged heart, pleading for someone to heal it.

I won't be the man to heal you, sweet one. I'm not your hero.

There were things in the brain that separated normal people from the insane. The amygdalae was one of them—two almond-shaped groups of nuclei that were located deep within the temporal lobes of a human's brain.

Researches had discovered that those two almonds processed memory, decision-making, and emotional reactions. In one study, monkey mothers with damaged amygdala displayed less maternal behaviors, at times beating and neglecting their kids. In another, men and women with borderline personality disorder had greater left amygdala activity than the sane patients. Even in alternative medicine, Buddhist monks that engaged in continuous meditation were able to strengthen that section of the brain.

That was why Asher mediated daily. He tried to fix himself.

Something had destroyed his amygdala. He had no proof nor confirmation from a head doctor, he just knew that something inside of his head had been damaged long ago.

Or do we really all love to kill? Am I one of the few humans on this earth that isn't denying their primal craving for death? Maybe, I'm really part of the normal group.

Death littered his past, blood too, as well as the corpses and the cutting of flesh right in front of him.

His mother patted the dirt with her shovel, slumped to the ground in an exhausted sitting position, and wiped her forehead. "Next time, we'll have to kill in a less gruesome way."

Shocked, a young Asher looked up from his tear-stained hands. "Next time? Mommy, we're going to kill again?"

"The best thing about. . ." His mother could not finish the sentence. She just gestured to the location of where her dead husband lay. "The best thing about your father's. . .accident is that I had put an insurance policy on him several years ago."

She shook her head and realized that her eight-year old son probably hadn't gotten the point. "It means that because your father is dead, we have the money to pay for the mortgage."

She gave him a weak smile. "We won't be kicked out of our apartment. We won't have to worry about where the bill money is going, whether to your father's gambling, liquor, or. . . even his filthy women." The last words she spat out with disgust.

Asher rubbed his eyes with both hands, as if it would transport him back to a normal day. "And Daddy won't hurt you anymore?"

"Exactly," she said. "So like I said, the next time we do this, it will be less messy."

She returned to burying his father's corpse, while Asher decided to not ask his mother again about what "next time" meant. Besides, four years later, he learned what she'd been trying to say that night.

Sometimes taking a person's life, solved the lives of many.

Asher shook the memory out of his head and returned to

the balcony, turning around right as Diana stepped outside.

Interesting.

He found her eyes first. They snared him. He had no idea what she wore or how her hair was done. The eyes kept his attention. He wouldn't be able to look away until he solved their mystery.

What is it about them that make me want to stare?

"What color are your eyes?" he asked.

She strolled over to him. "Most men would say 'hello,' 'how are you doing,' or even 'you look lovely tonight.'"

He smiled, captured her hand, kissed that soft skin, and gazed into those beautiful eyes. "Hello. How are you doing? You look lovely tonight."

"You're just dripping with suave this evening."

"Yes, I am." He drank in the rest of her.

Diana wore a red dress that brought out the rich color of her brown skin. He'd been around his mother long enough to know the gown's fabric, an expensive chiffon lace that fell to the floor, yet provided two delicious splits that showed off both of her legs to mid-thigh. The top was an empire halter with sheer beaded material swooping up, over her breasts, and around her neck.

His body did the expected things—heart beats picked up, his mouth salivated at the thought of yanking down the top of the halter and feasting on what lay underneath, his hands flexed in and out with hunger, and inside of his pants, heat warmed the area.

Maybe, she'll be more than an avatar. A play thing on

lonely nights. Nothing more. Regardless, it's show time.

"That is an amazing dress." He walked around her curvy frame and tried his best to study every detail of the material as it hugged her body. "This reminds me of the designer Hellen. That's Hellen with two l's."

She raised her eyebrows and said nothing.

"Yes." He studied the beading around her neck. "This reminds me of Hellen's Metamorphoses collection for this spring. Lots of daring gowns with artistic bead work. Hand-sewn genius."

She stared at him for a few seconds, not grinning or frowning.

Why hasn't she said anything yet? Is she not impressed? Why?

Asher had read that each person had automatic triggered responses for most things. If the person could incite a reaction by saying a particular thing, then one could figure out the ways to make that particular individual a puppet on his or her string.

In that situation, Asher had done the appropriate action to trigger the automatic response. He'd not only complimented her, he'd broken down the exact design of her dress and even the collection it came from. Most women would gasp or giggle as they stood in front of him stunned and impressed.

Not Diana. Why? Perhaps he'd come on too strong. Maybe she preferred subtly.

Too bad subtly wasn't his forte.

They both stared at each other for a minute. Although he

did catch her gazing at his body a few times in those silent seconds.

"I'm used to women looking at me for a long amount of time without saying anything." He shrugged his shoulders and came closer to her. "I'm gorgeous. This is the norm for me. However, it's also odd."

Again, she kept all expression off her face as she followed him with her gaze, analyzing and studying him with each step. "How is my staring at you odd?"

"You're not saying anything."

"There's nothing to say."

"I've just complimented you on your magnificent taste."

She held out her arms and did a slow turn. "I'm gorgeous. This is the norm for me."

"Awww. You're mimicking me."

"Or I'm stating the obvious."

"That you're gorgeous?" he asked.

"Yes."

"And what about my compliment of your dress?"

She formed her lips into a straight line. "Thank you."

He frowned. "Do you not like the dress? It's amazing."

"Of course it is. I bought it." She walked over to the balcony.

"And it is by Hellen."

"Yes." She glanced over her shoulder and flashed him a smile that made that area near his groin heat some more. "But you would know everything about women's fashions, being that your mother was a seamstress and dressmaker almost all of her life. Even designing her own gowns after husband number five."

He gritted his teeth and forced himself to maintain a neutral expression. His mother's past was something he exhausted loads of money and time to bury. The world knew of him barely ten years ago, once his last step father died, and he was announced as the heir. Before then, his mother and he had gone in and out of various social worlds with ease.

They never changed their identities. There was never any need.

The rich didn't ask many questions, assuming that their private clubs and exclusive residencies, kept all of the riff raff and killers away. The only problem was. . .that was exactly where murders loved to hide, among the wealthy.

That being said, no one knew about his mother's prior marriages. Every time she remarried, she hid the fact that she'd had any husband before. Any official that needed to be paid was given more than enough to keep their mouths closed.

"Fifth husband?" Asher asked through clenched teeth. "That's odd. My mother married my father. Yes. He left us when we were young, and then she married my step-dad, Mr. Gene Bishop."

"Hmmm." She watched a few yachts travel along the Cove's narrow entrance. "I think there's something you're not telling me. I'm particularly savvy when it comes to my research."

"Well, it seems your first line of investigating me has

resulted in a few mistakes."

"I don't think so. I have good sources."

Who would have been able to tell her?

"Have you ever tried to find your father?" she asked.

That question stirred the coldness in him.

Why would she ask me that? How much does she know? What did she find? Control the conversation. Get it back to where it needs to be.

"Are you not big on fashion?" I asked.

"Why do you ask?"

"Because you weren't impressed by the fact that I knew who designed your dress."

She laughed. "I'm sorry. Let's start over to where you originally broke down my dress to me with the aim of knocking me off of my feet."

She curtsied and then bowed. "Why thank you, Asher Bishop. You're such an amazing man! How do you even know Hellen? It's like you're this fashion-savvy women that lives inside of a gorgeous god. Never has a man taken the time to really look at what I picked out for him. Now I feel validated. Now I am woman. Now I can roar. By the way, can I have your children? Can we get married?"

Asher swallowed.

"Or would you like to look at my shoes first?"

He extended his hand. "Maybe, we should go back to 'Hello, how are you? You look lovely tonight.'"

She opened her mouth to speak, paused, and then shook her head. "You know what? I'm so sorry. I shouldn't have said that. I'm being rude for no reason."

She turned away from him and directed her attention back to the view. A breeze blew through her hair. A few wavy strands on the side of her face rose and fell back to her high cheeks.

"That wasn't rude." He got on her side and stared at the view with her. Moonlight and dimly lit yachts rode the ocean's surface. Giggling sounded below them.

"I'm sorry. My husband was brutally killed last night with his mistress. Tonight, I'm on a date. . .I mean. . .meeting." She closed her eyes. "Look. I'm an emotional mess. There are. . ."

She really is beautiful. And not in a right-in-your face sort of way. It's more her presence first, then her voice, and then those eyes. By the time, any sane man gets to the swell of her breasts and curve of that lush bottom behind her, he's probably already spiraled into madness.

She looked up at Asher. "Do you understand?"

It was in that moment, he realized he'd zoned out and had completely ignored everything she'd uttered.

"Yes." He nodded. "I understand."

What had she said?

"I'm more invested in this deal than I figured I would be," she said.

"Deal?"

"Your having me look into the serial killer, Cupid."

Shocked again for the night, he cleared his throat. "Cupid? You named the killer that?"

"Yes. The man or woman we're looking for is deadlier than we've thought. This person has killed eight people on Ovid Island at least."

Eight. How did she get that number? Only three others were connected by the police.

A knot built in his throat. This didn't happen to Asher much. The rich never paid attention. Sure, they played tennis, dined in high-end restaurants, chatted at charities, engaged in affairs, and gossiped all over designer hair salons and on the greens of golf course, but no one ever took notice of his activities before.

"Why did you say eight?" he asked.

"Five other rich white men were discovered in the past year. Although at the time, police never saw them as related. I have a person in the department who's working with me on this. He combed over ever Ovid Island death this past year, and found a few men that had been deemed death by accident or natural causes. Meanwhile, these same men had holes in their chest, thus confirming that the police on this island really are incompetent."

"Do you have a list of the possible new victims?"

"Yes."

"I want it, and any other information you can get me."

"Why?"

"I'm funding this. It should prove that I'm just as intrigued as you are." He raised one eyebrow. "What else did you discover?"

"I think I know Cupid's motive."

He stiffened. "Do tell."

"Well, maybe motive is too strong. I think I am understanding why he kills. He thinks he's protecting people."

Asher looked away and hoped she didn't notice, the awkwardness creeping around his eyes. This was supposed to be a fun evening, filled with quirky comments and titillating conversation.

He hadn't intended for Diana to peg him as adequately as she did.

"Mrs. Carson, I think you're jumping ahead of yourself right now. Maybe, it's due to the tragedy of this morning. Either way, I think we should just focus on the three murders, we're sure of."

"I won't argue against your opinion." She smirked. "I tend to go pretty fast when I investigate. Let's focus on the three murders, so you can catch up."

He ignored the slight, knowing that he'd probably deserved it. "Very well. Help me catch up, as you said. So, the police only connected three murders—Thomas Nickelson, owner of Lenwood Oil was the first body that they found with a hole in his chest that could be made with an arrow."

"Yes." She nodded. "Thomas was found in his daughter's room. This murder interested me more than the other ones, so I started with him first. I just kept wondering, why would Cupid kill this man, and then leave the dead body in the guy's daughter's bedroom. What was he trying to say?"

It took all of Asher's energy to keep himself still. This

was not as fun as he thought it would be. Earlier, he figured it would be interesting to get another's opinion on his secret activities, maybe play a little with the person's mind.

This was not fun. This was torture. And he had to endure it because he'd brought it all on himself.

Diana was just as good as his research had claimed. Although surely she possessed the face and body to climb up the new paper ladder of success, she'd done it with her brain.

Diana continued with her discussion, ignoring the tension that radiated from Asher's stiff frame. "My further investigating found that Thomas's daughter had confessed to friends that her father was touching her inappropriately. She'd also told another in secret, that she saw the killer."

"What?"

"She said, that night a man left her room right as she woke up and in the next few seconds, she spotted her dad on the floor with a hole in his chest—"

"Wait," he might've said too abruptly. "Further investigation? I met you this morning and am now seeing you this evening. You only had some of the day to investigate and already you have some witness's account?"

"Yes, the daughter saw a man. I talked to her best friend, a cheerleader for Ovid High."

Asher looked past her to calm down. "Did the daughter describe the man to her friend?"

"No. She didn't get a good look at him. She told the police that he wore all black, maybe a one piece or body suit. The room was dark. He had on a black hat too. She didn't get his hair color. She was only sure that he was white, but that's not hard to guess being that whites represent 85% of the island's population."

I didn't know the kid saw me. When did she wake up? I'm glad I didn't move Thomas. She kept tossing and turning. Plus, I hadn't want her to wake up to his dead body. Seeing your dead father is never good for sleep in the future. But, she kept tossing and turning.

"And then we have Jackson Mirabelli." Diana tucked some of her waves behind her ear. "He went upstairs with a woman who no one could find after the scene. The police originally assumed that a woman was involved. My friend got me the file to the case."

A weird darkness fell over him. He wasn't sure if he'd somehow shifted into the hunt or was drowning in unease. The urge to hurt something hit him, but he couldn't point out why.

"The investigation file?" he asked.

"Yes. I read over it today."

"You've been busy."

"Very."

She'd found eight of his murders in just half of a day, as well as got classified police files. What would she discover in months of investigating him? Maybe, this was a bad idea. Maybe, mother was right. I am a fool.

Asher wiped the sweat off of his forehead.

"I did several news pieces on Jackson a few years ago. One thing that the man loved besides drugs, was women.

Prostitutes to be exact. Ovid Island has its secrets, but most aren't well hidden." She winked. "I happen to know the madam of the most used sex service for the island."

He tensed in his suit. "Interesting. Did you find the woman that was with Jackson that night?"

"Yes."

His nostrils flared. "And what did she have to say?"

Diana hugged herself as if she was freezing. "She said a man came out of the closet of his bedroom, dressed in all black, and with a mask on his face. He held a bow and arrow, and pointed it at her."

"But he didn't kill her," Asher declared, more to push the fact that maybe Cupid wasn't that bad of a guy. "It doesn't seem like the murderer kills everyone, just certain people."

"Exactly. He didn't hurt her at all. The escort said that he told her she could leave, but that Jackson had to remain."

I should've killed her.

"Did she say anything else?" he asked.

"She said that she didn't get a description of him and truthfully didn't want to discuss it anymore. Absolutely refused to go to the police with the information, but. . ."

"But what?" Asher asked.

"She said that as she was leaving she heard the killer say something about how Jackson had hurt his sister."

Yes, I should have killed her.

"Then we have Neil." She walked away from the balcony's ledge and began to slowly pace back and forth. With each step, the bottom of her gown slid against the balcony's marbled floor and her heels clicked. "What I found intriguing was that Cupid never killed—"

"I'm sorry." Wrinkles crossed his forehead. "Why are you calling the murderer Cupid?"

"It's something that I do. I label the wrong-doers that I report on by whatever I think motivates them." She continued to pace. "It helps me stay detached from the person. If I know the killer's first and last name then I start thinking about who they are and where they come from. . .it all takes me out of the hunt—"

"Hunt?"

She stopped pacing and stared at him. "You interrupt a lot. Let me just go over Neil's death." She gulped in some air and then returned to the topic. "For the other two murders, Cupid didn't kill the survivor. Thomas's daughter and Jackson's prostitute."

She went back to pacing. "All evening while I got dressed, I kept wondering, why, over and over, would Cupid kill Neil's mistress, but let the other females go? Why not let the mistress go like he did with the others."

Asher leaned back onto the balcony's ledge. "I don't know. What do you think?"

"Cupid doesn't just murder people," she argued. "He has a clear, precise reasoning for why he takes lives. All three men were rich. All three considered harmful to females in some way. Thomas probably hurt his daughter. Why would a kid still claim that to her friend privately after her father's already dead? Because she's still dealing with the trauma of it all, that's what I think."

Diana sort of hit the air as if she was giving a low high-five to an imaginary person in front of her. "Thomas's prostitute said that Cupid said something about him hurting his sister."

"But we don't know if Thomas actually hurt his sister."

"It doesn't matter. All that matters is that Cupid thought that Thomas hurt his sister." Her pacing picked up, the gown swooshing along the floor and lifting a little with the wind. "Here we go again. We have a rich man that is doing something wrong to a female. Now go to Neil."

She stumbled for a second as if even thinking about her ex-husband was hard to do, like she was close to doubling over, if she didn't try to walk on. "Neil was married to me for several years. I'd caught him cheating many times. He also was emotionally abusive. I'm not saying that I'm this battered women. There are many wives all over the world that have been dealt evil husbands. And besides, some of it was my fault."

Perplexed, Asher tilted his head to the side. "How was anything Neil did to you, your fault?"

"I stayed."

"Most abused women do."

"I doubt that."

"Trust me. It's the truth." The sight of his father slamming his mother into the floor flashed through Asher's mind. He ran his fingers through his hair and knocked that image away. "Never blame yourself for the cruelty of a man."

"Still, I stayed with him, and that's not the point—"

"Why do you think you stayed?" Asher raised a blonde eyebrow. "Did you love him?"

She exhaled. "I stayed. That's all that is important to this situation. Regardless, Neil is another rich man that's hurting a female. So why would our serial killer hurt his mistress too?"

"Why do you think?"

"Cupid must have believed that the mistress was guilty too. She was his secretary on a small community of an island. She would've known that Neil was married, and could care less to sleep with him."

"That still doesn't explain why you call this man Cupid."

"Or woman."

He stifled in a chuckle. "Excuse me?"

"I still haven't decided if Cupid is even a man. Sure, we have witnesses that say otherwise, but I never rule anything out until the end. One thing is for sure, Cupid feels a certain need to protect females from harmful men. These are planned and researched kills."

Asher had no more words.

He was too busy being caught up in Diana. Back and forth, back and forth, she threw out ideas and thoughts without any fear of what it could do to her. Energy shifted around her. Things sparked in the air, or maybe it was just his imagination. Her face brightened with each rant. Eyes glittered with courage.

Luckily, the balcony door was closed, and the rest of The Cove's patrons dined inside, listening to smooth jazz and sampling on delicious food. They didn't hear the facts. No one would spread the news about his murders and get people's eyes opening a bit more.

Luckily, he still didn't think Diana was in danger of knowing his secret, that he was the killer, and thus in danger of dying right there on that balcony, in that lovely empire halter gown that fell to the floor.

Luckily, he didn't like to kill women.

Luckily, something inside of him urged to not kill her.

Luckily, she's so damn beautiful.

"Have you told all of this to the police yet?" he asked.

"No." She ran her manicured fingers through her hair. "Being a nosy reporter I don't actually have a good relationship with the police. I've been charged unrightfully for tampering with witnesses and evidence. I need something that I can really bring to them. I do have one friend there, now. I won't go to him with my thoughts until I have more supporting evidence."

"What about the two witnesses you talked to?" Asher asked.

"In the end, I won't be able to use either one of them." She turned around and walked back in the other direction. "I won't mess with Jackson's daughter. She's been through enough. And I'm sure that the prostitute that I talked to this afternoon has probably fled and is several thousand miles away from the island."

She better be, if she's smart.

"And although I told my one friend in the police center

about my own possible meeting with Cupid, I don't think he believed me. Why would he?" She ceased with the pacing. "I barely saw him. Truthfully, I'm not even sure he was even in the room when I. . .well. . .when I walked into the kitchen where. . .he'd probably been killing my husband right there."

She hugged herself tighter. "I felt something in that room. It was thick and hot and cold at the same time and. . ."

"What?"

"Alive. Electric." She covered her face with both hands. "I'm sorry. I know I sound insane. Besides, I haven't slept. Tonight was a mistake. I'm surviving off of my fifth cup of coffee. We should probably do this again."

Asher got up from the ledge, not liking where the conversation was now going. Funny how when she'd been slowly revealing him as a killer it had rattled him, but her possibly leaving . . .that fucking outraged him.

"Maybe, The Cove is exactly what you need." He took his time walking to her as if rushing her way would cause her unease. "Let's get you some food, an appetizer or if you have enough energy the five course meal I had planned for us. There's dancing inside and amazing music. They only hire the most celebrated artists."

"I'm sure they do, but this Cupid thing and everything else—preparations for Neil's funeral and—"

"Let's have you sit down." He captured her hand. It was warm against his skin as she curled her fingers around his. Energy sparked wherever she touched, shooting wickedness up his arm and down into his groin. "Let me take care of you.

If you're even too tired to walk, I'll lift you up and carry you in my arms."

In that moment, he crouched down to get ready to pick her up.

"Oh no." She backed up. "I'm fine. I just—"

"Yes, emotional wreck, mourning ex-husband, obsessed with Cupid's killings, and only running on coffee. You've listed a lot of problems, but you've forgot your biggest problem."

She looked into his eyes. "What's that?"

"It's been a long time since someone's taken care of Diana."

"I've always been provided for by Neil."

Asher might've stared too long at her, and even licked his lips right before he said, "There are ways that a real man can tell when a woman has not been taken care of properly."

He closed the distance between them, but didn't alarm her, by taking her into his arms, which he'd craved. "There are signs."

He tucked some of her hair behind her ear, just for an excuse to touch her, to feel the silk of her skin for a few seconds. "It's in the way she walks, the way she moves her lips to speak."

He bit his own bottom lip. "It's in her scent." He inhaled her, and Diana's eyes widened. "It's in the subtle sound of her voice, the way she looks away. . ."

She frowned. "Are you trying to say that I need to get laid?"

No, sweet one. You need to be fucked, so bad that you walk away from this investigating path. You need some dick to keep you busy.

Asher's cock grew in his pants. He did a quick check to make sure his jacket would hide it. "You need to be provided for."

"By you?"

"There isn't anyone else offering."

"How do you know?"

Because if anybody else offered to take care of you right now, they would be wearing an arrow in their chest. For now, others can stay away from you, until I've had my fun.

"I know what you're doing, Asher."

"You do?" Curiosity glazed over his eyes. "What am I doing?"

"Distracting me."

"Distracting you from what?"

"From being tired." She removed her hand and backed up. "I must apologize, but I have to go. Too much has happened. Goodnight, Asher." She turned around and walked away.

"Really?"

"Yes, really." She headed to the balcony door. "Maybe we can meet for lunch tomorrow."

"I don't want lunch. I want dinner, now."

She stopped and glanced at him. "Stop pouting like a baby. You'll get lunch tomorrow. I'm out of it tonight. I would be worthless for any more conversation."

"Maybe I'm done with conversation. Perhaps I want something else now."

"I'm definitely too worthless for that. And I'm a bit offended you think I'd give you what you want after one evening of wining and dining."

"Fine, Diana. Leave if you must."

She blew him a half-hearted kiss as if the gesture was only meant as a joke. "Fine."

"Additionally, I will be counting lunch as our second date," he called after her. "And will be hoping to get to second base at least."

"You'll be counting by yourself and holding your own balls and bat at the end of our second *meeting*, then. Let's try to remember that I'm a widower. It wouldn't be nice to take advantage of me in this emotional state."

But I will, sweet one, over and over again.

"Wait, Diana." Asher called out before she opened the balcony's doors. "You never answered my question."

She turned. "What question?"

"Why did you name him Cupid?"

"Oh," she sighed. "I figured that would be obvious. He kills with a bow and arrow, and all of his murders deal with some form of broken love."

And then she walked away, left Asher right there, baffled, and even more intrigued.

CHAPTER SEVEN

DIANA

Later that evening, Diana returned to her empty home, dressed in that elaborate gown, and exhausted from the whole day.

Asher Bishop.

Cupid.

Neil's murder.

There were too many thoughts circling Diana's brain and she couldn't settle on which of them to focus on. She wanted to think about Cupid and the onslaught of facts she'd learned in the last day, but Asher's blonde hair and blue eyes sliced through everything Cupid-related.

Though she would have to dress up in chic black garments, respectable but still fashionable black heels and stand over her late husband's grave in just a few days, Neil did not occupy the space in her brain as she thought he would.

It was easy to move him lower on the list.

Diana wished she'd listened to her gut a little earlier. Divorced Neil before he could tarnish the Carson name and bring her down with him. All things considered though, Diana knew she was getting a good deal out of his death. Money, attention, and pity. It looked good for her. Gave others something to focus their attention on, while she investigated Cupid.

Cupid, Cupid, Cupid.

He was an elusive little fuck.

She'd investigated, interviewed, and written about hundreds of murder cases during her news career.

None of them confused her like Cupid had.

She wanted to be disgusted with him.

Fear him.

But, deep down, she regaled him.

Celebrated the fact that he had balls big enough to do what so many were not willing to admit they wanted to do.

She wasn't even sure what she would do if she ever got a chance to meet him face-to-face. Kiss him? Pat him on the back with a "good going, mate?"

Diana shook her head while she stepped out of her designer gown. The chances of meeting Cupid were slim and would happen only if he was caught and then what could she do for him? Nothing more than help his tarnished reputation in the media.

She stepped toward the shower, letting the nozzle spew and spurt before the steam rose in waves toward the ceiling. The slate grey walls shone with a dewy glaze and it was in that moment, Diana thought the craziest thing.

How many times had Neil fucked someone in here? Who else had the pleasure of being in my shower, with my husband?

She stepped into the scalding water. Droplets hit her skin like ice picks.

What Neil had done, no longer matters. Get over it. He's dead, and with them, all of his mistakes. He's dead and none of his mistakes carry weight, unless they were related to Cupid.

And there it was again.

All roads lead back to Cupid.

Diana shivered as she remembered the feeling of stepping inside her kitchen. The way the air felt torched with electricity. It had to have been Cupid. There wasn't another explanation for it.

Asher hadn't thought she was crazy. She expected to see it in his eyes, the pity and disdain one feels for recent widows. But not Asher. He seemed to believe her. And she saw nothing like pity in his eyes—she saw fire. Little wisps of blue flames that burned right through her. He smoldered for her.

And she couldn't deny that she liked it.

It'd been a very long time since Diana Carson had felt wanted—in the way a woman should.

She was gorgeous, yes, smart and witty but that was all so surface level.

Men stared at her, wanted her, yearned for her, but none

of them *craved* her. None of the men she'd met, including Neil, had looked at her like they needed to satiate a hunger. She wanted a man to pursue her like it was a primal necessity. To ravage her slowly, surely, and then completely as if they would never have another like her again.

These were the fantasies Diana kept hidden in the furthest reaches of her mind.

Until Asher Bishop spoke and they fluttered to the surface like whispers of long forgotten secrets.

"You haven't been taken care of, Diana."

Water cascaded down her face and as she turned to grab her soap, a noise came from her bedroom. A small, imperceptible swoosh. Like shoes on carpet.

She ripped open the shower curtain but she saw no one. "Hello? Is anyone out there?"

No response. She heard no other sounds except the

drop,

drop,

dropping of the water stream.

She shook her head.

I'm losing it. I haven't slept or ate or closed my eyes once and this is the price I pay. And what the hell did I expect, if someone was in here? If they were in my home, then it was someone sneaking or planning to hurt me. I doubt they would've screamed back hello. God, I need to get a grip.

Wrapped in an oversized grey towel, she patted herself dry and the fabric lingered on her skin. There was a sensuality to it that had her stomach doing flip-flops. It was as if Neil's death had flipped a switch in her. The lingering pangs of desire she'd kept quietly at bay were now begging for release.

Tonight, I sleep. Tomorrow, I look for you Cupid.

She crept into her bed, the worn-in Egyptian cotton tickling her bare flesh. She hadn't slept naked in years! Not even when Neil decided to share it with her. She felt like she was newly divorced rather than recently widowed. The death of their marriage made sense.

The absence of Neil's life hadn't quite sunk in.

She clapped her hands and the lights shut off.

Silent minutes flew by.

Restless ones.

In the darkness, she tossed and turned against the coolness of the sheets for what seemed like hours. Her brain filled with images of men with holes in their chests, of Asher Bishop's charming smile and of Cupid's bow and arrow striking Asher in the heart. The image was so visceral, she sat straight up, clutching the space above her own heart.

And then she saw it.

A flicker of movement outside her window on the balcony. A swoosh of the curtains. A tiny clank of something on metal.

She rushed to the window, but of course, there was no one on her balcony. No man in a suit or one piece. No bow and arrow pointed at her. She moved away from the window just in time to see someone dressed in black turn the corner. She couldn't be certain if it was a man or a woman. A teenager or adult. She didn't even have enough time to see what he was wearing - just that it was black.

She laid back down and wondered if this was the end.

Perhaps it had been Cupid, checking on her. Making sure she was doing fine. But she wasn't sure he was that sentimental.

Wouldn't he be more occupied with his next kill?

Then maybe it was Asher.

Yes, I'm going insane.

She laughed, right there in the darkness, in the middle of her cold, lonely bed. A man like Asher wouldn't hide. He'd make sure she knew it was him.

But her skin prickled with the idea of it. That Asher, with his full lips and dripping charisma would come to see her.

She giggled as tingles moved from her fingers to her stomach and landed at her most sensitive part. Asher was right—she hadn't been taken care of properly. She hadn't been touched or fucked or treated like a woman in a very long time and she ached to feel it then. If only for a minute.

Her fingers moved of their own accord.

Down,

down,

down until her perfectly manicured finger tip rested against her clit.

It was unnatural for Diana to touch herself this way. Most often, she'd relied on Neil to satisfy her basic needs and when he failed, her vibrator did the trick. But that night, she'd wanted to feel it all. The touch of her own fingers moving inside of her. The rise and fall of her desire as she explored herself.

Yes. Take care of me, like you said you would.

She imagined Asher standing in front of her, naked.

How would his chest look against the glint of moonlight? Was he a smooth shaver like many of the rich men had become or had he retained his mark of manliness?

Her gaze roamed down imaginary Asher's body, taking in the deep v of his lower abdomen.

"Show me, how you'll take care of me." She hesitated before glancing as his cock.

She wanted to savor it.

"Show me." She pushed her finger inside of herself, deep enough to feel a sharp pain and then a waterfall of pleasure.

"Yes, Asher." The deeper she explored, the wetter she became. A warm slickness smeared all over her fingers. She alternated her speed from fast, twitchy probes to slow, thrusting thrusts.

Her voice came out in a sensual whisper. "Yes."

Only then, once she'd hit a level of desire she wasn't sure she could come back from, did she glance at the imaginary Asher's cock.

"Fuck yes." She wasn't a woman of exotic fantasies and unrealistic eight-foot dicks. She saw that he was average but thick. Not really long, but stretched out enough to please her every desire.

"Let me show you what a man does to a woman that he wants to provide for," the imaginary Asher groaned.

That thick, cock throbbed in front of her and she reached out to grab him, but pulled away when she hit the spot inside of her that drove her crazy.

"Jesus…" Her breathing increased with the desire coursing through her.

How had she never taken the time to do this before? Who needed a man when fingers were just as magical?

Asher's cock came back into focus and she so desperately wanted him then. She wanted to pull him into her mouth and suck his entire length, until he moaned for mercy.

She wanted him to fuck her from behind, his balls slapping against her ass.

She wanted him to taste her, every juicy bit she had to give.

Diana groaned as she came, her body wracking with mini-seizures. Her muscles tensed as she let the last part of her orgasm release and then she felt it.

The explosion.
The disorder of pain and pleasure, greed and gluttonous lust.
It all numbed her.
Made her shattered into nothing.
This zero state where she didn't really exist in the world,
Just on this plane
of
Sweet,

glorious,
nothingness.

CHAPTER EIGHT

CUPID

Through the window, Asher stood on Diana's balcony and watched her fall asleep. He'd come here out of the sheer urge to see her for a few more minutes. Breaking into her condo had been easy. Neil kept no real security, just some old guard at the entrance gate that had been sleeping when Asher climbed the gate and crept by.

His visit was only supposed to be a few minutes. Nothing more. A quick look, and then back over the gate, on the bike, and racing down the road.

But then she took off her clothes and stepped into the shower, and Asher could no longer think of why he would leave so soon.

Are you satisfied, sweet one?

How beautiful she slept after such a hard core orgasm.

Had she known he hid in the shadows, with his gaze hungry and plastered on her bare body? Did she sense the energy in the air, the same cold waves of power that sparked over his skin as she fingered herself?

He'd gripped his cock the whole time, at the first utterance of his name from her lips. He'd rubbed the throbbing tip, and yearned so badly to rush in and take care right there.

But he couldn't.

There was confidence in the hunting of a man, and then there was. . .

just plain old crazy.

Scaring the shit out of Diana as she masturbated in the shadows of her bedroom, would be insane.

No.

He waited.

Studied the groove of her body as it writhed in pleasure, and he hoped. . .

prayed that he'd be able to caress her exactly the way she touched herself.

Diana. Diana. Things are certainly going to change.

CHAPTER NINE

DIANA

Lunch on Ovid Island was as much an affair as dinner. If you belonged to the right crowd that is.

Diana took her spot beneath a creamy white umbrella, the frosted glass table set with matching daises, plates and linens. The waiter asked her what she would like to drink.

"I think I'll take a lemonade," she said, speaking lightly. The day before had been long and tiresome and though she'd done well to tire herself out with pleasure, a weary sensation dragged her down and kept her movements a bit sluggish most of the day.

"Are you sure you shouldn't get a coffee instead?" a deep voice sounded behind her.

There was no need to look back. She knew who it was, had imagined that voice in her ears all night. "No, I don't need coffee. I'm quite sure about that."

Asher came around to the front of the table and took a seat across from her. "You look like hell, Diana. I take it you didn't sleep well?"

"I slept well enough. And you, sir, are no gentleman. Haven't you learned how rude it is to comment on a woman's ragged appearance?" She pushed a tendril of hair in front of her face, that had been blowing in the breeze away from her face.

He smiled, though it was a bit forced. Much too put upon. "You're incredibly feisty, do you know that?"

"Of course I do."

"I figured as much." He gestured to the waiter, and ordered a gin and tonic much to her surprise.

Meeting Asher in the daytime, outside of her work environment was different than meeting him at night. Diana couldn't explain it, but it was almost as if he was reserved, docile, uptight during the day, while he let his guard down at night. She supposed that was the way for many, but she had neither the energy nor desire to change herself so rapidly. She was who she was—no matter what the time of day.

"You sure start early."

He waved her off. "It's never too early for libations, Diana. Now, tell me, how are you doing?"

Libations? Really?

"I'm. . .fine," she said.

"Ah. Hesitation. Tell me what's bothering you?"

How had he caught that? Was she that transparent? So see-through that this stranger, this man, could see right through her?

"It's nothing, really. My mind playing tricks on me. It's

just. . .I swear there was someone in my condo last night."

"You *think* there was or you *know* there was?" Asher leaned forward.

"Well I didn't exactly see anyone in my house. I heard something, like footsteps. And then when I went to bed, I thought I saw someone on my balcony."

The minute it crossed her lips, Diana laughed. "Shit. I'm losing it. This sounds so silly."

He reached his hand across the table and covered hers. "You *might* be losing it, but there *is* a murderer on the loose. Someone who knows who you are and what you do. This, Cupid, as you call him or her, might be aware that you're close to the truth. If your article caught my attention, why wouldn't it catch his? I don't think it's wise for you to be alone."

She laughed then, at the seriousness in his tone. The way his eyes commanded every ounce of her attention. "Oh, Mr. Bishop. Don't be so dramatic. You don't have to be polite and make up excuses for me. I know what falling off the rocker looks like."

He clenched his hand around hers. "First, it's Asher, not Mr. Bishop. I'm not fifty. Second, I'm not being dramatic. You're a walking target and don't seem the least bit concerned about it."

Diana pulled her hand out from underneath this. "Well, *Asher*, I've been around the block before. This isn't the first monster I've investigated."

"He's not a monster," Asher blurted out.

"What?"

"There's a difference. There are serial killers, and there are monsters. Some might be both, but just because a man is one, doesn't mean he's the other."

"Whether monster or just plain old serial killer, I'm not scared of Cupid, whoever he or she may be. It's obvious that the motive behind those kills are men hurting women and women hurting women. I'm not hurting anyone."

Asher rolled his eyes. "What's to say the motive can't switch to self-preservation? Who says Cupid won't kill you just to keep his identity quiet?"

"You did." She shrugged. "You just made a valid claim that Cupid isn't a monster."

"And what if I'm wrong? Do you need an arrow in your chest to think you might be in danger?"

Asher had a good point. But Diana Carson didn't run away in fear. No one, murderer or not, would push her out of her home, her job, or Ovid Island.

"Cupid is not after me. I truly believe that. I have nothing to worry about."

Asher gave her a look, part condescension, part concern. "As much as I'd like to believe you, I don't. Things are going to have to change. Are you ready for that?"

"Excuse me?" She sipped at her drink.

"You'll be moving into one of my spare bedrooms."

Diana spat out her lemonade. "You're kidding, right?"

His expression remained serious. "No, I'm not."

"Mr. Bishop. I mean, Asher, I'm not moving in with you.

I'm sorry."

The corners of his mouth tugged a little until a smile broke out. "Yes, you are."

Diana's fingers clenched into fists.

What the hell was wrong with this guy? He's crazy!

"Listen. I understand that you're concerned, and I appreciate it. I really do. But I'm a big girl. I don't need you, or any other man for that matter, to take care of me. I'm more than capable of handling myself."

"It's not a question, Diana. You are now an investment. The minute you agreed to our deal, I wired two million dollars into your Ovid Mutual bank account. It's sweet that you think I'm worried about you, and I am, but I'm more concerned with getting my money's worth."

Diana was speechless. Never had she been shut down with such intensity and command before. And who just dropped that amount of money for an investigation.

She needed to know more about this man, and how he would benefit from the capture of Cupid.

"I think that you've lost your mind," she said.

"Don't argue. It's useless. Just think about the advantages, Diana. Top of the line cuisine, room service if you wish, helicopter rides where ever your heart desires, and a beautiful lavish room as well as the best part, my company."

"Asher, I'm a grown woman who's taken care of herself for many years, way before I met my husband. I've reported news in the Middle East for gods-sake. I was in L.A. for some crazy gang shootings. I'm pretty good at protecting myself, and even more important, you will not boss me around."

He leaned her way and targeted her with his gaze. "Just say yes, Mrs. Diana Stubborn-Head Carson. Just say yes, before all of this gets messy."

"Excuse me?"

"I have many friends on this island that could make life difficult for you." He formed his lips into a slick grin. "The cops could deem the entire house as evidence and close it off for further use—"

"They opened the area already."

"I have friends—police that can bar you from your own property and lawyers that can tie you up in obligations to me." He leaned back, grabbed his napkin, unfolded it, and placed it on his lap. "I'm also pretty creative. Your boss could be included in this. Not to mention I have nothing but time on my hands. I could simply follow you around every minute of the day."

She crossed her arms and smirked. "You forget that I have a friend on the police force, too. I could get a restraining order."

"I have too many friends for that. Didn't I already say that?"

"Are you bribing Captain Rothschild?"

"I think the more important question is, who isn't bribing Captain Rothschild?"

"Not me."

"Which is why, you'll be forced to stay with me whether

you want to or not."

"Listen. Most women would hear all of these things, jump up from the table, and race away from you."

"You're not most women." He took a sip of his water. "You understand that no matter how ridiculous or overboard and creepy my earlier threats sound, the probability of me doing them are pretty high."

She raised her eyebrows. "How would I know that?"

"Because you're smart, and you know I'm invested in your well-being and working on this investigation." He shrugged. "You know I'm scared, and there's nothing in the world like a scared rich man. He'd surpass any limits to save his own mortality."

"So what you're telling me is that you're not going to let me say no about staying with you for a few days? Are you?"

Asher smiled, his dimples taunting her.

Diana's heart did something weird then. A little flip-flop. *Oh get ahold of yourself, Diana.*

"Mrs. Carson, I advise that you go home, pack up what you deem valuable, and be ready by seven o'clock this evening to be picked up by my driver. I'll have your room ready by then."

Diana couldn't believe it. What had her life become in the last few days? It was almost as if she were living in a movie. A strange movie where she couldn't figure out what would be happening next.

"You're exhausted." Asher pointed at her. "I'm well-rested. Say yes, now. Or we could go back and forth with this for the rest of the day."

"Asher—"

"Just say yes."

"But—"

"I won't let this go. Other things, sure. But not your safety, especially when it deals with my money. Just say, yes, for a few days. Think of it as a vacation, a long one."

"A short one."

"We can discuss the length of stay later."

"Or right now."

He rose from the table. "I'm sorry. I don't have the time to go over that. I suddenly realized that I have a lovely guest coming through."

"It will only be a few days at the most."

Asher stood up, and then flattened out his shirt and suit jacket. "See you tonight, Diana."

What just happened?

She said nothing and couldn't get up for several minutes afterwards. His scent and presence lingered after his departure. And for the tiniest of seconds, she thought she felt the same electric waves of air she'd felt in the kitchen the night her husband was murdered, and even the moment she'd been in the shower.

I should get this checked out with a doctor. Maybe I have cancer. Or a tumor. Or maybe I'm just fucking crazy.

Diana was the type of woman who trusted her gut implicitly. Even when she ignored it, it had never been wrong. And Diana's gut was bursting, whirling, and beeping out warning signs.

I'm going to stay with Asher Bishop for a few days. This is either going to be a giant disaster or a beautiful mistake.

Diana hoped for the latter.

CHAPTER TEN

CUPID

Books crowded Asher's mansion. They toppled his library and stacked the desk in his office. Nonfiction filled most of the shelves, although he indulged in many horror classics— Mary Shelly's *Frankenstein* to Stephen King's *It*, collections of Lovecraft to leather-bound editions of Edgar Allan Poe.

Asher read more than he slept or did anything else. He consumed words, did his best to memorize all the lines and statements on every page. Knowledge lived within books. It slept along the creases of tattered spines.

In medical journals, doctors presented ways to slice veins so precise, that no blood would spurt out and make a mess. Textbooks on social behavior, from psychology to marketing, taught the human mind's triggers and how they could easily be influenced.

And so he read, for years and many nights, in between the times he could satisfy his hunger for death. Books helped him cope with the thirst for blood.

Reading eased the dull ache in his skull when his mind drifted to his mother and her lovers… when he remembered the price he'd paid to save her.

That night he sat in his library and absorbed a book on the twelve steps to intimacy.

Diana had changed the level of the game on their first date. She was too smart to be easily impressed. He had to call in reinforcements. Everything rested on keeping control of her. She'd gotten a whiff of clues and witnesses in just one day and surpassed all the police's efforts to figure out the murders.

If she wasn't so beautiful, I probably would've thought she was dangerous.

In that moment, he realized he was falling into the same rabbit hole so many others had done before him. She was beautiful, yes, but she was fucking smart. So smart, she made men like Asher forget how distracted they could be around her.

There was hot lust that barreled in his chest, every time she came around him. He had to crush the urge in him to fuck her. He had to make her his between the sheets, just for a few nights. Nothing more. Just sex, and a taste, here or there.

He flipped a page and continued to read.

"And what is this?" His mother sashayed into the library and carried a martini with her.

She looked like she'd just stepped off of a soap opera set, one with big drama and wealthy characters. For hours, she would shut the world out, sip a glass of something wicked, and stare at the television. Asher never bothered her when she had them on, and never wanted to deal with her cursing and yelling because of it.

"Did you hear me?" She took her time sitting down across from him and sipped her martini.

"I'm reading about the twelve steps of intimacy."

"Why?"

He didn't even look up. "A behavioral scientist named Dr. Morris studied several couples and wondered why some stayed together while others divorced."

"This is not answering my question of why you're reading the book."

"I'm getting to that." He flipped another page. "So Dr. Morris studied hundreds of these couples and discovered that the successful, happy relationships had similar progressions of intimacy. They left a sufficient amount of time to advance to each stage. He theorized that with each slow progression in stages, it gave the couple a stronger bond."

"And the couples that rushed through all of these stages didn't develop anything?"

"They developed relationships, but their bonds weren't strong, and most usually divorced."

She set her glass on the table. "But why are you reading this?"

"It's interesting."

"Well," His mother crossed her legs. "I have another question."

He glanced up at her. "Are you going to let me read, Mother?"

"No."

"Then by all means, go ahead."

"Why are you sending me off to Paris for a month?"

He let out a long breath and returned his attention to the book. "I thought you liked Paris."

"I do."

"I'm giving you my plane and personal pilot. You'll have no limit in expenses. What is the problem?"

She frowned. "This sounds too good to be true. That's what the problem is, Asher."

"You've been stressed. I thought that you deserved a nice vacation."

"Is there anything else going on?"

He closed the book, kept it to his chest, stood up, and headed out of the library. "Goodnight, Mother."

"Why are they cleaning the west wing?"

"They? Who mother?"

"The staff, of course. They're dusting, vacuuming, and all types of things in the west wing of our home."

"They're cleaning that side for you. It'll be a nice interior design project for you when you get back. I'm hoping to have you work on renovations in that area, after Paris." He paused in the doorway and looked over his shoulder.

"You're lying."

"Why would I lie?"

"Is someone going to stay here?"

"Why would anyone stay here, Mother?"

"Do not talk to me like I'm crazy."

"I would never do such a thing."

"Why do you want me in Paris?"

"To shop, of course." He gave a fake yawn and backed away. "Maybe you can focus on finding interesting furniture and art out in Paris. Feel free to have fun. Grab several things. Be bold with your purchases." He grinned. "Put a nasty dent into our credit cards."

She frowned. "You're hiding something."

"There's nothing to hide, Mother."

She spat the next words out with sheer annoyance. "Don't mother me."

"Calm down."

"There better not be anything going on under my nose."

And with that, his patience withered away into aggravation. He grinned and targeted her with a scary gaze. "Or what? I better not have anything going on under your nose, or what?"

She glared at him, and he kept a neutral mask on his face. The times of her bossing him around had ceased after he killed the third husband. In those years, she'd taught him one important thing.

Death solved problems.

When he was a boy, she could shrill out a demand and he'd fall in line. But, he'd grown, and learned how to take a life and get over it with ease.

With her fourth husband, she'd seen the cruelty that Asher

could execute. By then he was a teenager, he'd captured the old man's neck with his bare hands, looked into his eyes, and watched the oxygen leave his body. His mother had asked him to kill her husband. She's claimed he raped her. But in the end, there was never any proof.

But by then, Asher no longer cared, when it came to murdering her husbands.

"Asher!" his mother yelled. "Are you paying attention to what I'm saying?"

He stared at his mother. "I am."

"No, you're not." She uncrossed her legs as if readying herself to jump up and attack him as she always loved to do.

I wonder if that old man ever raped Mother or if she just used it as an excuse for me to kill him. I wouldn't put it past her.

His mother flung her wine glass at him. He didn't flinch or move. Instantly, the glass shattered against the wall, right next to him. Pieces fell down to the library's floor.

Still, he didn't move, couldn't give her the satisfaction of knowing that she'd startled him. "Was that necessary, Mother?"

"You're ignoring me."

"I have a lot on my mind."

"Like what?"

"Business stuff."

"Elaborate."

For some reason, Asher couldn't get that fourth husband's image out of his face. "Remember, Mr. Anderson?"

She parted her lips and for a while remained silent, until finally saying, "My ex-husband?"

"Yes."

"Why are you bringing him up?"

"Did he ever really rape you?"

"Why the hell would you bring that up right now?" With shaking hands, she reached for her martini glass, realized she'd flung it, and then simply hit the table with her fists. "And why would I lie about something like that?"

"You wanted me to kill him."

"W-why would I make up a lie for you to kill someone? Asher, you have to stop blaming me for your own guilt. Enough is enough. You have all this guilt inside of you for no reason—"

He gritted his teeth. "We murdered men. That's why I have all this guilt inside of me."

"We murdered monsters."

"Did we?"

"Yes!"

"The only monster I remember was Dad. The rest," he shook his head, "I'm not so sure they were bad men after all."

"Hush!" She looked around the room as if someone might have bugged it. "We defended ourselves. That is it. Nothing more. These men hurt me and you saved your mommy. That is it. This conversation is over."

"They *all* hurt you?"

"Yes," she said through clenched teeth. "We've discussed this before."

"Did they all hurt you!? All five men?"

She jumped up. "Don't yell at me!"

He inched back and did his best to calm himself down. "I'm sorry, Mother."

She pointed to him. "You're not to kill anyone while I'm gone."

"I didn't have any plans to."

"No one dies, Asher. Do you understand me?"

"Goodnight, Mother. Enjoy Paris." He turned around and headed up the spiral stairs.

"And let the past stay in the past!" she called after him.

Each time his mother had asked him to kill her husband, she had a complex story that involved the man doing something horrible to her—rape, abuse, threats to hurt her son. Stories and blurry evidence filled Asher's childhood. She'd whisper their transgressions into his ears right before bedtime, tell him how horrible life was and how it would be so much better if that current husband was dead. Due to this, Asher never got too close to his step dads and did his best to stay away from them.

He didn't like to kill friends, and in the end, he always had to murder them.

Let the past stay in the past? That's easier for you to say, Mother. You don't have the guilt eating away at your insides. Did all of those men really hurt you, or did you just have me killing them for their money? Or did you get as hungry for death as I did?

Asher knew that only one of his mother's husbands had

been truly guilty. His father. He'd seen his father beat his mother night after night. At eight years old, all he could do was hide under his bed with his teddy bear.

Each time the angry man slapped her, she'd yell out for Asher. "Son, save me from your father!"

Under the bed, he'd cry like the little boy he was, not really knowing what he could do to save her. By the next morning, he'd wake up to her sleeping under his bed with him. Some nights they slept that way, under his bed and far away from the bad man that was his father.

The last time they slept under his bed, she faced him. Bruises covered her cheeks. Her left eye had been shut tight and coated with grayish-blue flesh.

Their father wasn't letting them out of his bedroom anymore and declared that both mother and child needed to learn an important lesson.

Monster.

"Mommy, I'm scared."

"I know, baby." Tears streamed down her battered face. "If he knocks me down to the floor again, you get the knife and slam it into his back as hard as you can."

Asher held his teddy bear tighter.

"He'll have the door open. You'll be able to run to the kitchen and get a sharp knife like the ones that mommy cuts the steak with."

Asher bobbed his head.

"You're the man of the house now." More tears came. "He's a monster. We have to kill the monster, Asher."

"Yes, mommy."

"Don't think about it. The monster needs the knife to go to heaven. He'll be nicer there."

Asher searched her face, not really understanding what she was saying, just hoping that he could really save his mommy.

And that was what he'd done.

That night, his father hovered over his mother, choking her as she flailed her arms out and hit the floor over and over to get free of his grip.

Eight year old Asher rushed to the kitchen, grabbed the knife, raced to his daddy, and slammed the sharp point into his father's back. Blood pooled along the hole. His father screamed and fell to the side, trying to grasp for the thing in his back, but he couldn't.

His mother ran into the kitchen, stumbling every few steps. She came back with a butcher knife.

And Asher didn't have to do anymore.

He just wrapped his arms around his teddy bear, stepped back into the shadows, and watched as his mother hacked away at his father and blood spray covered him, the walls, his teddy bear.

His poor,

poor

teddy bear.

He'd saved his mommy at eight.

He'd sent the monster to heaven.

But the monsters never stopped coming. His mother

married and married again. Each time, she found fault with the guy and needed Asher to save her. Each marriage, the man was richer and richer. By the fourth husband, he didn't care if the guy was a monster or not, he'd been too hungry to kill him the whole time they lived together anyway.

It seemed that Asher had discovered a certain taste for death and the color red.

"Mr. Bishop." Grace headed down the stairs right as he was climbing them toward his bedroom.

"Grace, how are you doing this evening?"

"Fine, Mr. Bishop." For some reason, her face appeared strained or tense. "I just had a few questions, sir."

He stopped on the stairs and tucked the book under his arm. "Go ahead."

"You want us to prepare the house for a guest? And I'm to add a place setting and provide grander meals? I'm sorry. I'm just relaying the instructions that I received from the house manager this morning."

"Yes. I had a meeting with house management. We will have a guest for a while."

"We will?" Grace formed her lips into a straight line.

"Yes. What's wrong?"

Grace tucked a braid behind her ear. "And. . .will this be a *real* guest or a. . ."

"As opposed to a make-believe guest?" He raised his eyebrows and wondered if Grace had started to doing hard drugs. From time to time, he'd caught a whiff of a smoky aroma from her shirt, but wasn't sure if it was his imagination or the scent of marijuana.

She cleared her throat. "I'm wondering if the guest will be...alive or...what I'm trying to say is...Will the guest be more like your mother?"

"A woman?"

Grace opened her mouth, but said nothing.

"I'm not sure what kind of question that is," Asher said. "But, I'm going to be patient with you and answer. Yes, the guest will be a woman, a lovely one at that, which means that if anything is out of place, I'll probably roar. Let's make sure everything is perfect."

"Okay." Grace still seemed unsettled. "And are we going to say anything about your mother?"

What is wrong with her? What kind of questions are these?

Asher crossed his arms over his chest. "Is everything okay, Grace? Are you having problems within your life? Is someone bothering you?"

"Oh what?" She touched her chest. "I'm fine."

"How's your ex-husband? Has he been doing everything he's supposed to? Paying child support and seeing the kids?"

"Uh, yes."

"Let me know if he stops or causes you and the kids problems."

"Um...okay."

"Anything else?" he asked.

"Uh...will your mother be meeting your *real* guest?" she asked. "Would I be making places for both of them?"

"No," he said with annoyance. "Mother is going to Paris."

The women in this place have lost their minds. It'll be good to have a fresh feminine presence in this household.

Asher walked past her and finished going up the steps. "Have a good evening, Grace."

CHAPTER ELEVEN

CUPID

Asher spent the rest of the evening reading his book.

12 Steps to Intimacy
Eye to body is the first step to intimacy. This is when a man first gazes upon a woman and really notices her for the first time...

Asher paused from his book and considered that moment with Diana. The first time he spotted her, she'd walked into a dark kitchen, not knowing the horror that lay inside. Asher had gazed upon Diana when he was really himself—bow and arrow in hand and blood all around him. No other women had ever caught his eye in that way. Most of the time if a female was around right before or after he killed, he'd either let her go, if she wasn't guilty, or take her life with the male monster next to her.

He didn't have to do that with Diana. She'd stepped into the darkness, sensed the electricity of him across her skin and backed away.

Too bad she hadn't backed away from him farther enough, because he'd started the first step to intimacy with her, right in that moment.

He returned to his book.

. . .Eye-to-eye contact is the next step. This is now active interaction between two people. Then we have voice-to-voice, where both people feel each other out. . .

Asher laughed as he thought back to his first date with Diana. She'd done more than feel him out with her words, she'd tongue twisted him, made him thirsty to taste her. That dress had snared his attention, her mind had caught his heart. And even the darkest side of him was intrigued with her fascination with Cupid.

I can't believe she named me that.

He grinned and returned to the book, scanning the pages for the steps that dealt with physical intimacy.

When does the touching begin and how do I get us there,

immediately?

    Eye-to-eye...
    Voice-to-voice...
    Hand-to-hand...
    Arm-to-shoulder...

Blowing out a long breath, Asher shut the book close and decided to make his own steps. With Diana inside of his mansion, there would be no way he could keep his hands to himself enough to slowly follow each step.

He wanted her now, could taste the sweetness of her flesh right on his tongue. He licked his lips at the thought.

I should go back over to her house and check on her.

His cock grew in his pants. His body and mind both knew that sneaking back over to watch Diane in her bedroom had nothing to do with keeping her safe. The only danger in her life would be her husband's killer, Cupid.

And he was Cupid.

I think I'm starting to like that name.

Asher unbuttoned his suit pants, stuffed his hand inside, and freed his cock. In his mind, he pictured the view from her balcony last night.

She'd been naked when she went to bed. Drops of water glittered along that flesh. He'd dug his nails into his hands just to keep him on that balcony and not diving into her room.

Her body lay perfect. Tight, dark nipples rose up and down on her breasts as she touched herself with such sensuality. She dripped with arousal and filled the whole room with that lush scent.

A hunger had rose in Asher.

His hands itched to dip his fingers between that wet flesh between her thighs. All that cream would cover those wicked digits. All of her. And he'd lick and lick it all the way, right before diving between those legs, lapping at her clit, and feasting on every inch of that warm pussy before his eyes.

That night, in the shadows of her balcony, he wanted to do more than fuck Diana.

He wanted to make her his—legs spread open, her screaming out Cupid, and him moving inside of her with enough energy to satisfy both of their hungers.

"I don't know what my plans are for you." He slipped his hands along his cock, stopped at the tip, and squeezed the throbbing point as he thought more of Diana touching herself. "I just know that no one touches you, until I'm done."

And there he sat in his bedroom.

Light bathed his half-naked body as he stroked himself and whispered Diana's name over and over. By then he'd gotten the tiny bottle of rose-scented lotion in his night stand and lathered his length with the perfumed cream. Sweat beaded along his forehead. He ripped his shirt apart to get more movement and be relaxed. His pants now hung at his ankles.

"Oh, Diana." His thighs flexed as he pounded his cock into his closed fists.

In his mind, she bounced on top of his cock as he lay on the beach. An ocean breeze whipped through her long, black hair. Those supple breasts bobbed as he thrust back into her. All around them the night air smelled of salted sea and sex.

"Oh, Cupid," she groaned.

And he didn't mind that she didn't moan Asher because, in the end, who was Asher?

Haven't I been a sort of fucked-up Cupid all along?

He stroked himself some more, groaning so loud he was sure some of the staff had heard him. He pounded into his hand, probably abused a finger or two, but he didn't care.

"Diana!" he roared and pictured her beautiful lips as she groaned Cupid again.

In several hot, tight seconds, his seed spilled all over his fingers and dripped onto the floor.

Still he couldn't stop stroking, not even when the lust trickled out of his cock, and the rim went numb.

When had been the last time he'd even satisfied himself this way? Sex tended to come out of need versus want. When he had the urge, he simply went to a club, picked someone up, took them to a hotel, and fucked their brains out.

Masturbation was never necessary, although he'd been

wanting to touch himself more and more since he bought the rose-scented lotion.

"Diana, you're in my head." Asher stared down at his now limp cock, wet with lotion and cum. "But I'll have you in reality soon enough."

CHAPTER TWELVE

DIANA

Diana sat in the back of Asher's limo, while his driver brought her to the Bishop Estates.

And what a sight to behold. Green, lush grass spread out for miles. When they passed the first entrance, three guards had stood in the booth and waved.

Rose bushes outlined the path as they continued onto Asher's property. A small pond sat on the right. On the left, huge trees had been manicured into perfect oval shapes and dotted with Florida's famed oranges.

Diana pressed the button on the side of her door. The window slid down, and she breathed in sweet, fruity air.

Besides the tires skidding along the road and the few birds chirping in the tree, the property held a natural quiet. It was a vibration of silent rhythm that held no real sound, but told the average person walking by that things were alive around them.

A peaceful bliss rose within her.

She should've been nervous, or at least taken aback by the past days horrific events as well as the uncertainty of each future day in front of her.

But she wasn't.

Instead, excitement skidded all over her skin, jumping around from pore to pore like tiny little fairies giggling and playing in spring.

Then they reached the second entrance. The limo paused as two security guards walked out of their booth, did a quick peek of the limo's back window, waved at her, and then gestured for the driver to enter.

A huge iron gate beeped three times and then slowly slid open.

He has some serious security happening. When did you get all of these men, Asher? Before or after you learned about the possible serial killer on the island. Are you that scared? Maybe you should be.

Suddenly, capturing Cupid rose to an even higher importance. Diana yearned for justice, just because it was the right thing to do when some crazy person took lives. She would've exhausted herself with this investigation, regardless, just for the simple fact that she lived on the island. Neil being a victim, propelled her need to find this guy. Maybe, putting Cupid away would get her some closer.

But now that she added Asher to the mix, things had gotten even deeper.

I don't want him to die by Cupid's hands. Asher deserves better. He's a good man.

Despite her desire to capture Cupid, there was a small nagging at the back of her brain that cautioned her. Cupid was doing Ovid Island a service, like a superhero. Who would rid the island of it's scum if he was caught?

The limo rounded the corner, and a massive mansion appeared right in front of her eyes and all her thoughts floated away as she stared at the architecture. It was made out of huge blocks of gray stone that had little flower and leaf carvings around the edges. Diana guessed the place possessed at least three levels and could probably provide housing for twenty large families.

Wow. And I thought Neil liked to spend money. This place is insanely big. Why have I never heard about this property? Why don't I remember meeting Asher before Neil died? Was he involved in the island society? He doesn't seem like someone that can stomach the people here.

Diana was no stranger to dirty, unrighteous wealth.

She'd grown up watching men and women steal, cheat, and even kill to gain their financial superiority. She couldn't deny that she had done some of the same things herself to get to the top. She justified it with her rags-to-riches past. The spirit of the tough streets always beat in her heart. She could never forget where she came from. Or the price she had to pay to get where she'd ended up. That mentality served her well, when she lived in rough places like Miami and New York City.

Ovid Island reeked of a different sort of toughness. If not for Neil, she probably would've never moved to the place, never been exposed to the disgusting gorging and spending of the elite.

Diana's first few months there, had been hell.

She'd been unprepared to live around the truly filthy rich. Instead of guarding her purse from the happen-to-run-by-pick-pocketers like she'd dealt with in Central Park, she had to protect her back from being stabbed by wealthy housewives with nothing to do. Instead of gripping her mace and looking out for attackers that crept in the shadows of South Beach, she had to guard her tongue and keep her cool, as evil CEOs tried to gag her articles and limit her reporting.

She'd had to claw her way through Ovid Island's upper crust society with only her intuition. Having several literary awards and a sparkling writing career didn't hurt either.

Maintaining her figure and classic look also worked. Instead of being looked down upon because of her dark, smoothened skin, she was reveled. Wherever Diana's face appeared, men took notice.

I should look more into Asher when I have time. I wonder who he spends his time with around the island? What clique does he run with? Who's back has he stabbed to get to where he is today?

From Asher's limo window, she stared out at the monstrosity of the mansion, and realized that maybe they weren't too different from each other, after all. That perhaps, their rise to glory was more alike than she wanted to admit.

The driver stopped, got out of the car, came to her door, and opened it. "Mrs. Carson, are all of these your bags, or will I be returning to pick up more?"

Diana gestured to her laptop bag, full of her computer, phone, and tape recorder for any quick voice notes. "I have everything I care about at least. Of course, there's some luggage in the back."

The driver punched buttons on his cell and talked into it. "Sir? Yes, she is here. Okay. Only a few bags, Sir. Okay. Yes. I will send Jenkins down to fetch the rest of her luggage from her home."

Excuse me? Who is he talking to? What do you mean the rest of my luggage from my house? I don't need that much stuff.

"Yes, Sir." The driver shut off his phone, and turned toward Diana. "We'll take care of your bags, Ma'am. Mr. Bishop is coming out to greet you."

"What did you mean about getting the rest of my luggage from my house?"

"I was told to get all of your belongings."

"But I have everything I need, right here."

"I understand."

"So you won't be returning to my house to get the rest of my things?"

"I regret that I must still go as per Mr. Bishop's orders."

Diana stifled a laugh.

He was so proper.

So rigid.

So… butler-ish.

I wonder what type of boss Asher is. Does he provide his

employees with more than just financial security?

"Okay, now I understand," she said. "I'll just handle this with Asher."

"Mr. Bishop will be out shortly." The driver went back to the limo.

Go back to get all of my belongings? That's silly. I only need a few clothes for a few days. There's no need to move in everything with me. He's absolutely ridiculous.

In front of her, the gigantic, wooden doors swung open.

Asher stood in the doorway, dressed as impeccably well as every time she'd seen him before. Black slacks hugged his long, lean legs. A white button down, formed nice against his muscular torso. He looked like the spitting image of goddamn Bruce Wayne.

If only we had a Batman to conquer Cupid.

She laughed then, as visions spun through her head of Batman with his expensive toys battling Cupid and his deadly bow and arrow.

"What's so funny, Diana?" Asher asked.

She shook her head. "Nothing."

"It doesn't look like nothing."

"Trust me. It's foolish." She waved his curious look away. "I figured you'd have work or some previous engagement since my move was such short notice. Were you waiting for me?"

His smile deepened. "Of course, I wouldn't let you spend your first night here alone. What a terrible host that would make me." Asher studied her belongings as his driver brought them to the door. "This only looks like enough for a few days."

"I only plan to be here for two days at the most."

"Diana—"

"I've thought about this and although your concern for my safety and your investment is nice, there's no real threat."

"He could be watching you, this Cupid guy."

"If he is going to come for me, it will be in the next few days. Until then, I don't believe I have anything to really be serious about. There's been no threats from him or even a substantiated break-in. You're basing all your fears on what I *thought* I heard, and it was probably just the wind." She looked around. "Besides, I think Cupid will be focused on his next kill, not some women that he probably doesn't even know or care to concern himself with."

Asher tilted his head to the side and grinned. "And you know this how?"

"His victims have always been men. I explained this already."

Asher wagged his finger. "And what about Neil's mistress?"

A pang hit her heart. The reminder of her husband's death along with his adultery still hit home at times. The wound from both were still too strong, it sat within her, festering at times, when she was alone in the emptiness of their place.

"I already explained why Cupid murdered Neil's mistress. He thought she was just as guilty as Neil."

"And you're willing to leave the safety of my property in

two days, on this guess?"

"No."

"No?" He quirked his eyebrows.

"I'm going to stay with you for two days to give *you* time to gather a proper security team with all of that money that you put into my bank account."

"Why thank you, Mrs. Carson. I always like to know my orders ahead of schedule. And who is the security team for?"

"Me. You'll be providing this team for me."

"And is this my only option of keeping you safe?"

"Yes."

"I'm not sure I agree."

"Doesn't matter. And I've discussed this with my boss, just in case you want to use him as a threat. My boss and I both believe that this funded investigation is important to the island and beneficial to the paper. However, we also agree that a security team is more rational than an Ovid Island news reporter living under the roof of one of the wealthiest men on the island."

His face shifted into a neutral mask. "Well, this is a twist."

"Is it?"

"Yes. It seems my guest will only be here for two days."

She beamed. "That's correct."

"Stop it." He frowned.

"What?"

"You're over there grinning like a child that's stumbled upon their parent's secret place for hiding Christmas presents."

She shrugged. "My mother and father never could find a good place to hide the toys. I always found them a good week before Christmas. Luckily, they wrapped all of them before hiding them."

"You never opened any of the presents?"

"No way."

"Not even a little peek, like pulling the corner of the wrapping paper back just a tiny bit? Seeing as how curious you are, I don't believe you. Not one bit."

"No. The goal was never to ruin the surprises. I only wanted to outsmart my parents."

"And I bet you did," Asher said. "As much as possible."

"Since I only have two days with you, let's start now." He captured her hand. The heat radiated from his palm and warmed her down to her bones. He chuckled to himself, as if he understood the effect he had on her. "Are you sure you won't reconsider, staying longer?"

"I can't. Remember. I have funeral plans as well as so many other things to get done."

"You have the money to hand all of those things down to a staff."

"If you want something done right, you have to do it yourself," Diana said in a sing-song voice.

Asher's left eyebrow rose. "Touche. A woman after my own heart. However, you really should consider pawning off your tasks. Then you'll have time to stay with me, the loneliest man on the island."

Diana eyed him. A wealthy, god-like man with good taste, good manners and the fortitude to go above and beyond for his investments.

How is he lonely? No way. But wait a minute, why is he still single? How has no one trapped this good-looking man?

He cleared his throat. "Diana?"

"I'm sorry. What?"

"Stay with me for a week, at least."

"I can't."

"You can."

"How about we finish this conversation later, and you show me around?"

"Fine." Asher pulled her inside and it was as if Diana stepped into a fairytale.

Diana darted her gaze around the house and couldn't settle on what to be transfixed with first. The high ceilings? The bay windows that overlooked Ovid Island? The cream and gold walls that sparkled at every angle? There weren't a lot of things that surprised Diana anymore, but this house?

She was completely in awe.

Asher winked at her. "I take it you find your accommodations sufficient?"

Diana couldn't answer him. She was too busy staring at an archway covered by intricate iron bars with a huge door blocking the way.

"Where does that go to?" she asked.

"Ah. A woman with a perceptive eye and good taste. That would be the way to the wine cave."

"Wine cave? You're pretty serious about your wines."

His lips curved into a salacious smile. "As every well-educated man and woman should be." He pulled her forward, through the grand entrance of the kitchen. "I have the best chef on the island here. Her name is Grace. She'll make you anything your heart desires. All you have to do is ask."

He paused for a minute and sighed. "Although she's been acting a little odd in this last year, so if all your requests aren't met, just let me know, and I'll talk to her."

Diana stared at the commercial size kitchen. For as much silver and granite she could see, there were twice as many people shuffling around, doing God knows what.

"All of this is for you?"

"Not *just* for me."

"Wouldn't there be a lot of food wasted each day?"

"Not here." Irritation glittered in his eyes.

Diana considered stopping the topic right there, but decided to push it a little further. For whatever reason, mentioning the waste annoyed him. She liked that. Most didn't care. Almost all, ignored the fact that they were filling their garbage cans with pounds of untouched gourmet food every day, while people all over the world starved.

"I'm just saying," she continued. "This is a huge place and there's a lot of food being made. You're only one man."

He ceased with walking and spun on his heels. The rest of the words came out in a careful tone, but Diana could tell that she'd definitely hit a nerve. "Unlike the other people on this island, I'm not that selfish or crazy with my spending.

Whatever's cooked in this kitchen feeds all of the staff. They're never denied a meal. Never."

"Hmmm."

He didn't move. "Hmm?"

"That's good."

"But not good enough?"

"Look." She raised her hands in front of her. "We're off topic, and supposed to be doing a tour of your home."

"I feel like your questioning my contributions to society."

"Really? All I said was that your kitchen staff is making a ton of food."

"Yes, but it came off as something more. So let's deal with this now, so there isn't any confusion." He placed his hands into his pockets. "Last year in Miami, the homeless shelters had begun charging people to stay and eat there. For each person, it cost ten dollars a day to sleep on a tiny cot surrounded by a hundred strangers—old and young women, mothers fleeing from domestic violence just hoping to keep their kids safe, addicts lost in their own reality. Ten dollars a day to stay there."

"That's madness."

"That's not all. In order to eat in the soup kitchen, it cost a dollar with every meal."

"To our associates on this island, that's a humble deal." Asher stepped close to her. "But to you and I, that's wrong. We know damn well that if a person's only choice is to sleep in the streets, to walk around homeless, then there's a huge possibility that the person doesn't even have the money to pay the shelter."

"You're right."

"So I changed that. I paid everyone's bills, took over ownership of each shelter, built another one focused solely on mothers and kids that for whatever reason were forced to live out on the streets."

She gulped. "Why are you telling me this?"

"Because, you saw the wealth around me, and figured I was just like every other man on this island."

"And you're not."

"No, I'm not."

"Sorry," Diana mumbled.

"That's fine." He took her hand again, but she pulled away.

"I have another question."

He raised one eyebrow. "And what is that?"

"Why the focus on mothers and their kids?"

"Why not?" He captured her hand, but she refused to walk forward. "What?"

"Answer the question."

"I did."

"No, you gave me another question." She twisted her lips. "Why the focus on mothers and their kids?"

He smirked. "I believe the children are our future—"

"Really?" She interrupted him. "You're going to quote a Whitney Houston song?"

"Fine. I have a special passion for helping mothers and children out."

"Especially ones dealing with domestic violence?" she asked.

"Why would you say that?"

"You were the one who mentioned it, Asher."

"Did I?"

"Yes. You brought up that there's a lot of abused women in homeless shelters."

"I also mentioned drug addicts."

"Yeah, but that's a typical stereotype. But, most people wouldn't think to bring up the fact that a lot of shelters are filled with broken families."

"I'm sure that's common knowledge."

"I don't think so."

"I'm sure of it." He pulled her away, and she decided to leave the topic alone and follow him. In her head, more questions rose.

The best way to know a rich man's insides, is to see how they spend their money. Buying up all the shelters in Miami and even building his own for mothers and kids trying to escape domestic abuse? That's not some passion that you happen to pick up. That's an ache that came from. . .unfortunate things. Did he see someone being hurt in his childhood? Was it all around him? Where did he grow up? What was his childhood like?

For the remainder of the tour, Diana barely heard half of the things Asher said, as she swam around the thoughts in her head.

Minutes flew by with each step. Asher guided Diana

down hallway after hallway filled with polished walls that led to room after room of stunning furniture and exquisite art. A haunting magic thickened in the air. She half expected the candlesticks and clocks to come alive.

Each space held its own scent. The kitchen radiated savory aromas. The bathrooms emitted flowery fragrances. The bedrooms roared with herbal perfumes that tantalized the senses.

Yet, for some reason, the whole mansion made her feel like she was walking through a high-end hotel, instead of someone's home. The place had the right scents, look, and sounds, but no warmth flowed through the air, just this stiff, coldness.

Is he really alone here? I would be.

There were other odd things that set Diana on edge.

In every room, a large oil painting of what she guessed to be his mother hung on each wall. On every one of her portraits, clear, blue eyes stared back beneath a bundle of blonde curls that were usually stacked high on top of her head. She was an attractive woman, and there was no doubt that Asher had gained his gorgeous looks from her.

Maybe, in these two days of staying with him, I can get a closer look into who he is. I still never figured out what he would gain out of funding this investigation. Sure, he would be safe from a serial killer, but what else? And what's up with all of these paintings of his mother?

When Diana had researched Asher, there hadn't been any pictures of his mother. Which was surprising. Most affluent women relished in flashing cameras all around them. Additionally, the few articles Diana discovered had been difficult to find. She'd called in more favors than she should have.

For that first meeting at The Cove, she'd wanted to prepare herself for Asher, surprise him with the depth of her knowledge on him. So she'd delved deep into his history. Though there was no indication of murder, malice, or wrongdoing in his life, Diana found some details hard to swallow. Her research revealed all of Mrs. Bishop's marriages. Something that Diana didn't think most of Asher's society friends were aware of. She'd bribed too many just to get that tiny bit of data. Someone had paid even more to keep the woman's history buried.

Who wanted to keep her marriages a secret, Asher or her?

Mrs. Bishop had been an unlucky wife. Each husband died a few years after the wedding, leaving Mrs. Bishop in a pile of wealth.

To most that would've seemed odd. For the rich, it was pretty normal for a beautiful young woman to marry a rich man, and he die later. Most of the ambitious women wedded the old and sickly, then once their husband died, they married again. For the wicked female, wedding the rich was a career.

And besides her first marriage, Asher's mother had been at least twenty years younger than all her ex-husbands after.

There was also absolutely no information on Asher's father. That concerned her. In a few interviews that Asher had done, he'd discussed the fact that his father had left him and his mother.

With all of his wealth, why hadn't Asher sought his father's identity out? Or had he searched for him and just didn't want to confess such a private thing to Diana or the world?

Throughout the whole tour, Diana tried to keep her questions to herself. But after the tenth room with a huge portrait of his mother, Diana could no longer stifle her urge to bring the woman up. "So these are paintings of your mother?"

"Yes." He guided them out of the study. "She likes seeing herself in every room."

Still, I don't think I would have kept them up after she died.

The last article on Asher's mother was her obituary. She'd died in a huge fire on the Bishop grounds. There'd been no police investigation or anything further.

Maybe Asher will tell me more about what happened. Well, that's if he was comfortable enough to reveal it to me. God, listen to me. I'm always on the story. Leave this alone, Diana. Cupid is the one I'm supposed to be focused on, not Asher Bishop. Who cares about his past?

Diana followed Asher as they walked down the hallway. "And now that your mother's gone, you keep the paintings up in her memory."

He captured Diana's hand and led her up the stairs. "She's never really gone."

She's never really gone? Even though it's been years, it must still be too difficult to heal from.

An hour later, Asher showed her the last room.

Hers.

It was spacious with a king bed, a luscious armoire, walk-in closet, and big windows that looked out onto a field of pink roses. The bathroom was connected and the deep slate cream marbling on the floor stunned her.

"This is captivating," Diana said under her breath.

"Would you expect anything less from such a captivating man?" He asked her.

"I guess not."

"Everything is here for you, and more."

"More?"

"Whatever you need?"

"I don't need much."

"Then, whatever you want." He licked his lips.

"I don't want much."

"You should."

"You're a woman that deserves to be taken care of."

"That's right." She tapped her forehead. "I forgot about that."

"One should never forget the fact that they are desperately in need of getting laid."

She laughed then.

It was unexpected.

She hadn't laughed in months. And the timing? Terrible. But there she was, staring at Asher with a *feeling*. An emotion she couldn't quite put her finger on. She didn't want to find out what it was either. She had more important things to focus on.

"Well. . .I'm exhausted. Thank you for the tour and the accommodations though I still believe I don't need them."

Asher looked at her—no, that's wrong—he looked *through* her. Like he was trying to find all the secrets she locked up tight. His gaze moved up and down her body, a laser of appreciation that she couldn't ignore.

Diana swore if he spent one more second looking at her, she'd burst into flames.

She'd crumble like ashes at his feet.

But, he looked away and edged back. "It's getting late. I'll see you in the morning."

"Right. See you in the morning."

Asher closed the door behind him and Diana flew to the bathroom to cool off the heat rushing through her skin.

There's no way I can do more than two days. I'm glad I decided not to stay longer.

She turned the nozzle to frigid. She needed to shock herself out of whatever was coursing through her. She stuck a hand out and the water was paralyzing. It did the trick, for a few seconds.

Asher. Asher.

She stuck a foot under the stream and every burning thought of Asher slipped away. All she could focus on was the shock of frozen droplets pricking her flesh over and over again.

"Finally," she said aloud, shutting the nozzle off and walked into the bedroom.

Sometime during the bathroom break, all of her bags had been stacked in the corner, but she was too exhausted to deal with them. Diana wanted to close her eyes and float away into slumber. She undressed and slipped under the duvet and moaned when her skin met with silk sheets.

"Damn you, Asher." The silk caressed her flesh like a lover's fingertips. She shivered against the cool fabric, imagining how she must look in the big bed by herself.

And that thinking, brought her back to thoughts of Asher.

What does he look like in a matching bed with similar glorious sheets? What would he look like in this bed, with me, naked?

Heat pooled between her thighs.

No, no, no. I will not masturbate to this man, while lying in his bed.

Asher was not part of her plan to solve the case of Cupid. He was her funding, yes, but he needed to stay out of her way. She couldn't have him invading her space or her every thought. She needed to be clear-headed and focused.

Maybe, I can think about this more. . .after the investigation. . .after Neil's funeral, and all the problems that have come from his death.

She shut off the lamp on the bedside table. Darkness spilled around her. There wasn't a sliver of light anywhere and for a moment, Diana was frightened.

What if Cupid came to kill Asher and he believed she'd

done something wrong? What if Asher was right and Cupid was set on revenge? Had Asher really taken all the proper precautions to protect them from this madman who was set on destroying the rich men of Ovid Island?

Stop it right now. You are Diana fucking Carson, not some scared little girl.

The rising tension in her shoulders evaporated into nothing. She believed in her voice of reason. Relished it. She *was* Diana Carson, a great reporter and the person who would blow Cupid's identity right open.

And as Diana fell asleep with images of bows and arrows and gaping holes in chests, a visceral thought came to the forefront.

She was going to lure Cupid out of hiding.

Her plan could be a simple one.

Not too complex.

She just had to talk it over with Asher.

What if we got an actor or someone to be Cupid's bait? What if we got an actor to pretend to be this rich guy on the island that harmed females? But then who would volunteer for that? No way. Cupid was smart. He wouldn't believe that.

Another thought hit her.

Asher could pretend to be the bait, but then that would put him in harm's way.

Would he agree to that? Probably not. But it could be something that worked.

Scenarios littered her mind. Tons of possibilities kept her awake. With Asher's money and willingness to help, somehow, she would catch Cupid red-handed.

CHAPTER THIRTEEN

CUPID

I said more than I should have.

In his secret security room within the mansion, Asher leaned back in his chair and stared at the monitors in front of him. Every room had a hidden camera in the ceiling. The bedroom that he'd put Diana in, held four.

On the television screen in front of him, Diana slept in her bed. Shadows and moonlight bathed her. Due to the night vision cameras, the images glowed in a green hue.

Something is on her mind? What is it? Cupid or me? She didn't seem like she was scared at all, when she argued about only being with me for two days. But, something is clearly bothering her.

For several more hours, he watched Diana toss and turn in the big bed, whispering something out loud whenever she woke out of her sleep for a few seconds.

"What's bothering you, Diana? Did I say too much?"

Diana rolled over and placed her back to that camera.

Annoyed, Asher directed his attention to the other tv screen on the right, that now showed her sleeping face.

"Two days. That's all." His hard cock ached at the thought. He'd been erect since Diana arrived, and wasn't sure his length would ever go down. Clearly, watching her on the monitors wasn't helping.

Every cell in his body screamed to go fuck her.

"Fine. Two days. That's all I need." He gripped his cock, but refused to rub or stroke it.

It's bad enough that I've been watching her in her home, and now mine. I won't start jacking off to her like a complete sexual deviant.

For the rest of the night, he held himself, but didn't do anymore. Diana rolled over a few more times, and even whispered his name on her tongue.

And, like an active volcano, violent flames lapped at his core.

Hours passed.

He didn't sleep.

He just watched her like a mad man, heating up even more until he could've sworn that sweat beaded along his forehead.

This isn't enough. I want to smell her too. I want that scent in my nose for the rest of the night.

So he rose from his chair, left his hidden room, shut the door, and headed upstairs to smell Diana.

She can't catch me doing this. She'll think I'm a

creep. . .as she should.

CHAPTER FOURTEEN

DIANA

Diana opened her eyes and was face to face with Asher. She let out a yelp before hugging the covers to her chest. "What the—"

"Sorry." He sat on the bed right next to her with the oddest look on his face, part madness, part pure enjoyment.

A shiver of fear and. . .even weirder, lust shot to her veins. She formed her mouth to speak, and couldn't gather her words.

"It's eight o'clock." He showed her his watch. "I figured you for an early riser. I was worried."

"You were worried?" Diana scrunched her face together. Every minute she spent in Asher's presence got stranger and stranger.

"Yes, I was worried." He ran his fingers through his already disheveled hair. It looked like he'd been disturbing those curls all night, just messing with his head due to worry or whatever obsession he had.

"So. . ." She made note of how close he was too her on the bed.

How long has he been sitting here? How long was he watching me sleep? Was he watching me, or did I wake up, right as he sat down?

He cleared his throat. "I should probably go."

She looked at what he had on.

Wasn't he wearing that yesterday?

"How was your sleep?" he asked, without getting up or moving away.

"More important," she gestured to his day old outfit. "How was your sleep?"

"I didn't go to bed."

"Clearly." She let out a nervous giggle. "Hopefully, you didn't stay up all night, sitting in here, and watching me."

"Yes. Hopefully." Heat lingered in his gaze. "That would just be crazy."

"Yes," she muttered.

"Regardless, I didn't get much sleep last night, but then, as they say, who needs rest anyway. I can sleep when I die."

Something imperceptible fell over his face as if he wanted to both cringe and laugh. Diana thought she knew everything Asher was about, but she was figuring out how very wrong she was.

"So. . ." She took her time, sitting up. She'd worn nothing to bed and only slept under a thin sheet. It barely concealed anything—providing a lovely view to Asher of her shape and so much more. Even worse, her dark nipples had stiffened with hunger and were presently poking at the thin material over her chest.

She cleared her throat. "So."

Asher stared down at her breast and inhaled the air in front of him. "So?"

"I'll just get ready and meet you downstairs?"

"Okay." He didn't move. His gaze stayed glued to Diana's chest. She felt stuck, naked under the covers with Asher staring at her like he wanted to devour her.

"Asher?"

"You are a very beautiful woman. Did you know that?"

Diana pursed her lips together.

His behavior was odd, but he was being nice—more than nice—but it also made her squirm to be under his watchful, judging eye. Plus, she probably had bad breath and morning hair. She didn't think beautiful was the right term for him to use.

"Um, thank you."

"You're aware of what you do to men like me, yes?"

Diana shifted beneath the covers and held them closer to her skin. "Are you referring to the intimidation men like you feel in my presence?"

Asher laughed and it shook the bed. "I'm sure you intimidate many men, but no, Diana, you don't intimidate me. You fascinate me."

"How so?" She asked, a small but recognizable desire expanding in her belly.

"Your eyes light up when you talk about hunting Cupid.

You're dedicated to your job. And those lips appear to be deliciously kissable and yet. . ." His voice trailed off making Diana wonder what he meant to say.

She needed to hear the rest of his words. The burning desire was beginning to work its way up her limbs. "Yes?"

"Let's just say, you should be kissed and by someone who knows how."

Diana arched her eyebrows. "Why, Mr. Bishop, you couldn't come up with anything more exciting than a well-used line from Rhett Butler?"

Asher didn't laugh or smile, he just looked at her with intensity raging in his eyes. "Although a fictional character, Rhett's words don't mean any less hundreds of years later, Diana. He meant them to Scarlett and I mean them to you. You're a woman who deserves more than . . .what you've been given."

"You barely know me."

"I know enough." He leaned his head toward hers and captured her mouth.

Oh my God.

Diana's body waged a war inside of her. Her brain told her to stop him. To remember the craziness of him being in her room like he was. She wanted to pull away before their lips became forever intertwined, but the

thump,

thump,

thumps of her heart told her to stay still. To let Asher Bishop kiss her like she'd never been kissed before.

And he did.

His lips smashed into hers and every vein inside of Diana thrummed.

Every sensation,
every sound,
everything was amplified.

There was magic in a man's mouth.

Asher traced her jawline with his thumb. Like a thirsty man, he yanked away her sheet and cupped her right breast with his other. Jesus, he was fast.

He knew what he was doing.

He knew how to rile Diana up without even fucking her.

He'd been right when he made the statement at The Cove. She had never been taken care of properly by a real man, never experienced a kiss like his before.

An all-consuming hunger filled her stomach, lungs, and heart.

She starved for him, desired more and more.

Asher pulled back and Diana's sheet lay in her lap, exposing the top half of her body to him. Those perky brown breasts greeted his eyes.

Diana didn't reach to cover herself back up. Her nipples and everything else were his for the taking, in that moment and he seemed to consider it.

But instead of taking her right there, he reared back, a

scowl lining his face. "I'm sorry. I shouldn't have."

"What?"

"I'm sorry." He jumped up, his hard dick pushed against his pants and caught all of Diana's attention.

She wanted to touch it, see his cock in real time, instead of imagining it over and over in her head. "What do you mean, you're sorry?"

He edged away from the bed.

"What's wrong?"

And then he raced from the room.

Diana opened her mouth, and for the second time that morning, had nothing to say.

In one second, Asher had been on her bed, devouring her lips.

In the next second, he ran out of there like his cock was on fire and he needed to plunge in a tub of water.

He was there and then he wasn't, and Diana wondered if it had all been a dream. A sick, twisted dream that she suddenly wanted to be reality.

She pinched herself hard, and yelped, "Okay. So that crazy shit really just happened."

No, it had not been a dream. Asher Bishop had just woken her up, kissed her as no man had done before, and then ran away like a creepy person.

She fell onto the bed.

This situation with Asher gets crazier and crazier.

CHAPTER FIFTEEN

CUPID

He ran away, because he was scared.

It didn't matter that there was no logic in his reasoning.

It didn't matter that she probably thought he should be committed to a mental facility.

He just knew that he couldn't touch Diana anymore, without giving up a part of himself.

That morning hadn't start like he'd planned. He'd hoped to seduce Diana, not kiss her like a teenager, and then run out the room like some virginal jerk.

That wasn't how it was supposed to be.

Asher avoided Diana the rest of the day, skipped breakfast, and headed to the office without leaving her a message.

I'll come up with some explanation later. She probably thinks I'm crazy. And what about her saying that she'll only stay for a few days. No. That can't happen. I need to know what she's doing to me.

The kiss changed things, made his heart beat faster and his hands tighten around her body as he held her. Asher hadn't wanted to let go, and that scared him the most. All of his life a treacherous woman ruled his days and ordered him to do horrific things. Well, not anymore.

He wouldn't have another woman with that much power over him.

All I want to do is taste her tongue again, just one more time. I just have to be more in control, next time I touch her.

Yet, Asher hid in his office and piled himself under work all day. He couldn't sit in the mansion with Diana, walking around and spreading her presence all over the place.

She smelled so good, I sat by her side all night, breathing her in the whole time. That can't be one of the twelve steps of intimacy, the step where the man hovers over the sleeping women and sniffs.

Last night, he'd been unable to get control of himself. Her scent alone had him stroking himself.

While she slept, she had no idea what danger lay next to her. The things that played in his mind, scared even him. He'd thought that killing had made him hungry, that the smell of blood was an adrenaline rush.

He was wrong.

Diana called to another craving inside of him that he'd ignored for far too long. For the rest of the day in his office, he was famished, and couldn't pin point why.

How many women had he brought to his bed? How many

faceless rich girls had he stuffed his cock into and smeared his cum all over their happy, welcoming lips? He fucked and moved on to more interesting things like his bow and his arrow, and the thirst to cover them both in blood.

Then Diana came.

She walked upon him, late in the night, shielded in darkness, and stepping right onto his own beautifully orchestrated death scene.

He'd been intrigued by her that first night.

Once he read her article on the deaths, he knew that she was smart, someone he could have fun with. Make a game of it, he thought.

No. This isn't going like a game should. I'm not winning, and I'm not sure she is either. We're both just wandering crazily around the board.

The phone rang in his office and brought Asher back to the reality of his day. Without thinking, he picked it up. "Hello?"

Diana's sexy voice traveled over the line. "You've been hard to contact today."

He tensed in his seat. All the words he'd considered saying, left him. Imagine that. A killer scared of some tiny woman on the phone.

Why do I care so much about looking like a fool in front of this woman? Why would it matter?

He cleared his throat. "How are you doing, Diana?"

Maybe, she won't even bring it up.

"I'm fine, but a bit confused."

He gritted his teeth. "Is the spiral staircase giving you trouble?"

"No."

"What about my chef Grace? Has she prepared—"

"Grace has been amazing. Although she seemed a bit shocked that I was there. I don't think she thought I really existed."

He sighed. "Grace knew you would be coming. I don't know what's going on with her these days. She's been weird."

"She's not the only one in this house that's being weird."

Diana is not going to let this morning go. Why can't she just ignore it?

Asher feigned ignorance. "Are there other people on my staff that have been giving you problems?"

"Why did you leave, after you kissed me?"

He covered his face with one hand. "I. . ."

"Yes?"

"I. . ."

"Okay?"

He shrugged. "I haven't exactly come up with a good reason for why I left like that."

"Then what is the truth?"

"I prefer a well-thought out lie."

"I like honesty."

He took his hand away and leaned back in his chair. "No, you like facts."

"Aren't facts and honesty the same thing?"

"Never. Especially not in our world."

"Our world?" she asked.

"The land of the rich."

"You're avoiding my question."

"I'm really good at that."

The line went silent for a few seconds before she finally replied, "Would you like me to return to my house? I was only going to be here for two days anyway and it's clear that —

He jumped up, accidentally knocking over one of the many pictures of his mom that sat on his desk. "You don't leave."

"Excuse me?"

"I mean." He calmed himself down. "I want you to stay. This morning was awkward because of me. You did nothing wrong."

"I thought maybe—"

"Trust me. Whatever you're thinking is wrong. I'm much more complicated than you could ever dream of. If you can remember that, then. . .we'll do just fine."

"I'm still only staying for two days."

"I need more time."

"What?"

"I mean. Cupid is out there."

"Asher, you have more to be worried about than me. You fit Cupid's profile more than I do. Remember. He likes to kill rich men that break female's hearts."

"Well, I haven't broken anyone's heart yet."

"Let's hope that you don't in these next couple of weeks."

Asher didn't like the worry in Diana's tone.

Did she think that he could hurt her? Never. He could hurt others for her. He knew that was possible inside of him. Part of him wished another man was out there named Cupid and stalking her. He'd love to search him out and slice the deranged guy's throat.

Without thinking, he blurted out, "I won't hurt you."

She made a sound that traveled over the phone, sort of between a sigh and gasp. It was as if she'd been holding in air the whole time and finally let it go.

"Will I see you tonight or are you going to be hiding from me all day?" she asked.

"I plan to only hide until dinner, so yes, you'll see me tonight."

"Good."

"And. . .as far as your stay at my house—"

"It's only going to be two days, Asher."

"Okay. I won't push it."

"I'll see you tonight."

"Yes," Asher said. "I'll see you later."

He sat on the line for the last few seconds, until she hung up. In that moment, he exhaled, and hadn't realized he'd been holding in his breath.

What is she doing to me?

As day shifted into the evening, the moon replaced the sun and the island came alive.

Workers crowded transport boats and headed home to Miami's mainland with dreary eyes. They left in hoards—painters, day maids, masseuse, nannies, and on and on.

The rest of the island remained in a constant buzz of excitement. Warm air shifted to a cool breeze that rustled all the palm trees. Sweet smells filled the air, from designer perfume to the savory aroma of roasted meats. Giggling sounds rode the wind. Men headed out on the streets with heavy pockets and sexy women on their arms. Tennis rackets and golf clubs also got good use that evening, clacking and booing at they slammed against balls. Champagne glasses clinked at country clubs and high-end restaurants. The theater sparked alive and enjoyed packed seats. Some of the hottest celebrities came to perform each evening, and that night was no different.

Asher should've gone straight home that night. Surely, a beautiful women sat at his table, waiting for his company.

I need more than two days with Diana. I'll fix that first, then I'll fix that kiss that I messed up this morning.

Diana believed she was safe. It didn't matter that she was right. What he had to do was guarantee at least a week with her. There were too many questions rising in his skull, too many things happening within his chest.

It had started after that kiss.

No, it had started long before that. The moment she walked into that kitchen, she meant something to Asher.

In his head, a blackness had spiraled over and over just like the huge staircase in his mansion. After the kiss, the steps broke in some places. Things warmed where it should have been frigid, cold. The gloom in his core vibrated. That had never happened before.

He pressed his mouth against hers, and he changed.

If just a kiss could do that, then what would her body do to me?

In his limo, he sat in the back. He'd ordered the driver to take him to a secret address, one that only a few men knew.

I need more than two days.

What he was about to do would be dangerous. He hadn't thought it all out, and had planned on going straight to his house.

But, Diana believed that she only had two days with him, that there was no threat. Asher decided to change that.

She needs to be scared, and in my house for a little bit longer.

None of this made sense. Even as the driver parked him in front of the concealed brothel, he still wasn't so sure he was doing the right thing.

I have to do something.

His driver got out, walked over to his side, and opened

the back door.

"Thank you." Asher nodded at him. "I'll be back in an hour or so."

The driver said nothing and returned to his post.

What am I doing?

To any wanderer, the property that sat in front of him appeared to be a normal three-story house. Multi-colored tulips bordered the whole place. A swing hung from a tree. It even had a white picket fence around it.

Asher put his leather gloves on his hands, placed the black mask on his face, and headed down the lit path where music wandered out to him and mixed with feminine laughter.

Only a few knew what happened in this place.

It had taken him several months to be invited himself. After playing a long round of golf with some other CEOs that lived on the island, one fat meat head out of the group slipped him a black square of paper with the address written in gold.

"What's this?" Asher asked Len Gibson, the meat head who sat right next to him at Ovid Country Club's bar.

"You're a pretty quiet man, Asher." Len waved for the bartender

"I am."

Len turned to Asher and winked at him. *"I know why you're quiet."*

Asher grinned. *"I doubt that."*

"Men like us have pleasures that others. . ." Len leaned in closer and whispered. *"Basically, other men might not be*

able to stomach the things we like."

The bartender didn't even ask for Len's order as she placed a tiny glass with brown liquid in it, right in front of the fat man. Len grabbed it and took a long gulp.

Asher had no idea what the man was talking about as he rubbed the gold numbers and letters with the pad of his thumb. "So this place provides these. . .pleasures that most men couldn't stomach?"

"Yes."

"And how do you know I like these things?"

"I saw the way you were looking at Thomas and his daughter." Len took another gulp of his drink and chuckled.

"What do you mean?"

"You know what I'm saying." Len nudged Asher's arm.

Asher held back the bile in his throat. "I think Thomas may be a bit too friendly with his daughter. That's why I was looking."

"Is that the only reason?" Len nudged him again.

It took everything in Asher to not break the man's arm. Instead, he directed all of his attention back to the address on the paper. "So this place, provides those type of services?"

"I might have taken Thomas there a few times, but the girls aren't you know. . .young enough for him."

Darkness hit Asher's chest. Haunting images ran through his mind. He could see himself killing Thomas, even though hadn't planned on hurting anybody else that year. He'd already killed two men prior, but then he spotted Thomas placing his hand in the corner of his daughter's back.

Although the action seemed simple, there was something wrong in the way the man looked at his little girl and smiled.

And her eyes...

He'd never forget the terror that lay beneath those lids.

It was why Asher sat at the bar in that moment. He'd been trying to decide if he would kill Thomas, and maybe Thomas's death would get that terror out of his little girl's eyes.

"Yes, buddy." Len got up from the bar and tapped Asher's back. "This is the place to have a little fun with a younger grew of women. They're still mature, of course, just not by society's ridged standards. I hope you'll see me there one night."

Asher knew exactly where he would place the bow in Len's chest, could see the sharp object slicing through the air, slamming into the fat man's flesh, and bursting through to bone and blood.

"Thanks." Asher formed his lips into a huge smile and shook the man's hand. "I really hope I catch you there too, Len."

He'd never got down to killing Len. There were too many others that snared his attention—too many piece of shit men to kill.

Asher decided to kill Len, when the urge just couldn't be stopped.

That night, it was a full moon.

Asher hadn't realized it until he stepped onto the brothel's porch and gazed out into the sky. The stars shimmered around that huge, glowing object. Power rained down and bathed

Asher in it.

I need two more days with Diana, and, besides, Len should die.

He placed his club membership key into the door, twisted it, turned the knob, and stepped into the brothel. Inside, two bodyguards glanced at his mask, and then returned to their conversation.

This wasn't his first time.

He'd had several drinks with Len this past summer, watched the man walk off with young girls a few times, and did his best to keep himself on the bar stool, night after night, and not do anything about it.

He had to be careful then, but not tonight.

Things had changed.

Diana had come to his life, and named him something more.

I'm Cupid, and Cupid would've never sit around for this long, as little girls got their innocence taken away from them, night after night. Diana would approve of this kill.

Shadows danced all over the walls as he traveled through. Men wore masks like him, as well as the women. No one wished for their identity to be known. Too many bad things happened there. Too many naughty men filled the empty spaces of the house. There were so many secrets that could get out and no one wanted that.

The brothel had been designed like the ones of western days. Satin draped all of the rooms. Candles seemed to be the only way light could be used. Piano music played everywhere.

In minutes, he arrived at the back of the house where a small bar rested. One big fat man with a huge black mask sat there, guzzling down a small glass with brown liquid, and talking to a female that couldn't have been more than fourteen.

Hello, Len.

Although a lace disguise covered her face, her arms were tiny as well as the rest of her body.

"And so I signed the merger." Len slammed the glass on the bar and returned to the tiny girl. "That's life. Some people get money. Others have to sacrifice so that those people can get it."

"You're not worried about what this could do to your worker's families?"

Maybe, this girl is older than fourteen. She sounds smart.

"Sometimes the blood of others can bring pleasure to a few. Is that so bad?" Len asked.

She just gave him a weak smile and sipped her water.

Asher tapped Len's shoulder. "Speaking of blood and pleasure."

"Is that you, buddy?" Len turned to him.

They didn't use names here. It was always a *buddy* here or a *friend* there, nothing more. Besides, no one ever took off their masks.

"We should go upstairs and talk." Asher waved the bartender away, when she approached.

"Upstairs?" Len whispered.

"I have an interesting business endeavor, something you would definitely be interested in."

Len considered Asher's words for a few seconds and got up from his seat. They'd hung out by the bar many nights. There'd be no reason for Len to be alarmed.

"Will this make me money?" Len asked.

"Would I bring something to you if it didn't?"

Len chuckled and hit Asher's back. "Yes, you are correct, buddy. I only go into things unless it makes me cash. That's the only way."

They walked away from the bar together. Asher glanced over his shoulder to check the girl. She remained behind and was no longer looking their way, probably happy to be rid of the fat man.

Through another darkened passageway and then up the stairs, the walked together, side by side, and whispered.

"These other men here," Len gestured at a few walking by, "They were born with money. They're not like us. We worked hard to get here."

"Well, you are the only one who worked hard. I got my share through my mother's marriage."

"Trust me. I know that racket. Surely, you had to grin when told and suck in any discomfort around dear old step daddy."

"Something like that." Asher thought back to all of his stepfathers and stifled a laugh. All of the men had feared him. They probably didn't know why, but it was something in their guts. None of the his mother's husbands could sit around

Asher for too long, no matter what his age was.

Had they smelled the blood on his hands? Did they see the horror in his eyes?

Asher and Len arrived at the last room on the third floor. No guards existed this high. There was a special price to pay for this access. This floor was for people who loved to do bad things. Cameras were shut off, at least that was what the establishment promised.

It didn't matter to Asher.

If they recorded what he was going to do with Len, then let them.

They didn't have his identity, and even if they somehow figured it out, they knew he would expose them all. He had the money.

And besides, Len's death wouldn't be the first one on this property. Others had killed here before. Rich men had stabbed competition among this hallway. Celebrity actors had mistakenly gone too far with some of the girls.

Secrets remained here, while the corpses were delivered in neutral tone boxes at the doorsteps of the dead person's home, with no explanation to how or why it had gotten there.

This has to give me more than two days. Hopefully, if I make the crime scene gruesome enough, they won't put Len in a box. They'll get scared and call the cops to come. Maybe even pretend like the establishment is on the up and up, if they're not already bribing the police.

They stepped inside Len's personal play room. The fat guy had boasted about it when he purchased it last summer.

"Oh the things that I've done in that room." Len had laughed. *"It will keep me out of heaven for sure."*

"Do you really believe there is a heaven?" Asher had asked.

"God, I hope not."

And then both men laughed, one found his own ironic joke funny, the other chuckled at the image of killing the comedian in his head.

Only moonlight seeped into the room and gave the space a little light.

Len walked in. Asher closed the door. Both of their images stared back in the mirror across the room. Chains and leather straps dangled from the ceiling above his bead. A table sat on his right, stacked with wooden paddles..

"I think there's a lamp over here." Len got ready to head in that direction.

Asher grabbed his fat arm and stopped him. "No. We don't need light."

"What?" Len chuckled and stared at Asher's hand on his arm. "Hey, buddy. You're acting a bit weird."

"Sorry about that." With his free hand, Asher grabbed the knife and pulled it out of his pocket. "By the way, how many girls have you had up here?"

"What?"

Asher brought the knife to Len's view.

Could the man see it? Probably not.

Asher hoped he could.

Hoped the man was pissing in his pants.

"What's that in your hand?" Len asked.

"Your destiny."

"Wha—"

"Destiny." Asher slammed the sharp end of his knife into the bottom of Len's chin. The blade sliced through his flesh. Blood sprayed onto his mask.

"Sorry, buddy." Asher leaned back so it wouldn't get in his eyes. "What a mess."

Len struggled as he died, jerking his arms and lazily fighting to get out of Cupid's arms. It was no use.

"This is why I hate using a knife." Cupid slid the knife out and hammered it into his chest over and over. Each time, the sharp edge met bone, a bang sounded.

"It's so loud too." Cupid let go of Len.

The fat man fell to the ground.

Cupid crouched down. "You were supposed to feel the pain of my arrow, but I had to improvise tonight."

Len's body violently shook.

In the shadows, dark liquid gurgled from all of the holes that Asher had made.

"You see. There's a girl, but isn't that always the case when someone dies." He dropped the knife onto the carpeted floor. "She's more than I thought she would be."

He grabbed the dying man's shirt and snatched it open. Buttons flew. A few hit Cupid's chest, but he paid them no mind.

"She's beautiful, but that's not why I like her." He ripped through Len's holy and blood-stained undershirt. "She's smart, but seriously, the world is filled with smart and beautiful women. It's why I can't read those god awful romances."

Len's head bobbed a little, his hands lay limp on his sides, while his legs jiggled every few seconds. The odor of death filled the air and Cupid inhaled it all.

"I mean. Isn't the world filled with beautiful people? And any reasonable man or woman could argue that at least half of these gorgeous individuals are smart." Asher tore away more of Len's shirt and stared at his chest.

The moon bathed the punctured skin in a glow of light.

"Plus, most of those chick flicks are boy meets girl, boy does something stupid, girl finds out and leaves, boy somehow gets her back." Asher picked up his knife and studied Len's chest as it slowly rose up and down.

Somehow the fat man still held on. He had a few breaths in him. His heart continued to beat just a little bit more.

He's still alive, a little. Good. I'm going to enjoy this. Can he hear me? Too bad all of the little girls he stuck his prick in, couldn't see his death.

"But then I met Diana." Asher found bare and unpunctured skin at the area right above Len's fat pecks. "Our boy meets girl story was very different than the norm. She happened to stumble upon me doing my night time pleasure. The sort of hobby that you sadly happened to stumble upon tonight."

He brought the sharpened edge of the knife to Len's chest and carved out a C. The body shook, but there wasn't much energy or life left in Len to stop Asher.

"So now we have me dropping right into some sort of romance story." He finished the C and went to the U to continue spelling his name in Len's chest. "I'm the boy. Diana is the girl, but what I will not have is that same formula. No. Our story will be something more."

He drew the P, I, and D. "The girl will fall in love with the boy and not get mad. Personally, I doubt the boy will take her being mad at all."

In the moonlight, he gazed at his bloody name on Len's chest. "I haven't figured out how I'll keep her, but, tonight, I think I just realized I want the girl around me more."

Maybe, more than a week.

Finally, the body went limp with death.

Asher gathered up some of Len's blood, went to the door, and wrote:

To Diana with love. . .

Thinking of her, he dragged Len's heavy body to the door and propped the man against it.

"There we go." He sighed. "That has to give me another week at least."

His phone buzzed. It was probably Diana, wondering where he was. Next time, he'd have to make sure he had a good albi.

He took off the gloves, stuffed them in his pocket, and answered the phone, "Hello?"

"Are you standing me up again?" she asked.

"Again?"

"You left after our kiss. I'm counting that as a stand up."

"I don't think that's fair." Smiling, Asher headed over to the window, lifted it up, and climbed out.

How many times had he left this way? For weeks, he'd planned how to take Len's life. Things had gotten in the way. Other men's murders came easier, and then there was his mother.

"Are you coming?" she asked.

"Yes, I'm on my way now."

"Good."

He paused on the window's opening. It would take him time to climb out and then connect to the tree that leaned toward it. The branches were an even harder trick to accomplish, although he'd done it many times, ripping his pants and getting a cut here and there on his leg.

"Diana?"

"Yes."

"Tonight, I'm going to kiss you."

Although he couldn't see her, he knew she was grinning when she said, "And should I attach a rope to you just in case you run away?"

"No, My Love. But we can use the rope for other things." He hung up before she could reply, stuffed the phone back in his pocket, and got ready to climb down.

Wait a minute.

He froze right there in the moonlight.

Did I say. . .my love?

CHAPTER SIXTEEN

DIANA

Diana wasn't sure what came over her. The minute she stepped foot in the Bishop mansion, every secret desire she'd buried deep in her subconscious burst out of her. She felt as if she'd been living as a subdued, cocooned version of herself but then Asher came along and…

What was it about that man that changed her? He was sexy and delicious but it wasn't his looks that did her in. It was more, the way he dripped with intellect and secrets with the curving of his lips.

Perhaps it was the way he demanded control from her in the most pleasurable of ways.
And that kiss,
it had broken something inside of her.
She'd tasted his lips,
delectable,
addictive.

She hadn't wanted him to stop,
and when he ran away,
rage and shock bit through her.

How could he leave her with only the whispers of his cologne and the heat of his hand on her cheek? He wouldn't get away with it again, she would make sure of it.

Every thought she had about Cupid ceased to exist the moment she decided she would fuck Asher and get it out of her system.

If she could just satiate the hunger blazing through her, then maybe she could focus on more than the way Asher's voice made her want to explore what was beneath his expensive suits and shiny ties. She wanted to know everything she could about the man sworn to protect her. The man who told her exactly what he was going to do to her and when.

"Tonight, I'm going to kiss you."

She'd bitten her bottom lip and touched herself then, though she worked very hard to keep her voice calm and steady on the phone. She'd made a joke to keep the playfulness going, but then his comment about the rope threw her off and she was thankful he hung up, because she cried out in fervor.

"No, My Love. But we can use the rope for other things."

She sincerely hoped he had a rope on a standby, because suddenly the idea of being tied up while Asher thrust into her over and over again gave her shivers.

Diana slipped out of her clothes, every last stitch of fabric. She picked up the phone extension in her room and pressed 0 for house management, as Asher had instructed her last night.

"Miss Carson, what can I do for you?" a woman asked.

"Um, yes, I need you to bring me one of Asher's most expensive button downs. White, please."

"Oh...his button downs? Mr. Bishop?"

"Yes."

"I'm not sure if we're authorized to do that."

"Trust me, when I tell you this. You'll be making Mr. Bishop a happy man if you do this for me."

Silence hung on the line for a few seconds, and then the woman replied, "Okay, Mrs. Carson. We'll get the shirt for you."

"Please, hurry." She hung up the phone and checked her watch.

Asher would be home any minute and she was going to surprise him.

Maybe, I should've asked house management for a rope.

A few minutes later, a knock came.

Excited, she opened the door a crack to hide her nakedness.

A short red-head woman handed the shirt through the small place. "Here you go, Mrs. Carson."

"Thank you so much." Diana grabbed the shirt, shut the door, brought the button-down to her nose, and inhaled.

Jesus, the man has refined taste.

His signature cologne teased at her nose. If she had to guess, the fragrance was made from some earthy scents, like teakwood and bergamon oil.

She closed her eyes and let the soft fabric glaze over the flesh of one arm. Then the other.

"Let's see what I look like with it on." She closed the shirt around her, and stepped in front of the mirror.

Her dark skin shone brilliantly beneath the white of the shirt and she admired the desire oozing from her. This was a Diana she hadn't seen in a long time, and she welcomed her home.

Lust boiled inside of her and she couldn't wait to see what Asher did when he saw her.

Sorry, Cupid. You're hunt will have to wait till tomorrow.

She considered all of the many reactions that Asher could have to her nakedness under his shirt. Would he devour her right there on the spot? Would he freeze her burning veins with slow, tepid kisses down her torso until she begged for his cock?

She shivered and slipped into her heels.

There you go Cupid. You get one more day to be free of my investigation. This is my gift to you. You did me a favor. You led me to Asher, and no matter whatever comes from him and I, I know it will be interesting at least.

A half hour passed, and Diana waited for Asher in the foyer with one leg crossed over the other. She'd arranged herself enough to hide all her juicy bits and when the time was right, Asher would see her as everything she was.

The ancient clock in the foyer ticked by and chimed at nine o'clock on the dot, and not a minute later, footsteps sounded down the hall. Asher's voice came next, as he talked to one of his staff members, told them goodnight, and then rushed toward his grand, spiraling staircase.

Diana cleared her throat. "Good evening, Asher."

He snapped his head in her direction and she wasn't sure if it was lust, pride, or greed she saw in his eyes, but he froze right there in his spot. "You're. . ."

"Gorgeous? Witty? Brilliant? The queen of your existence?"

"Yes. All of those." His gaze moved down to the gap in the shirt, where Diana's breasts were on full display. Again, her hungry nipples hard craved his attention.

She gestured to the sneakers at the end of the step. "You see those?"

"Yes." He studied them for a moment, and then returned to drinking her in, his gaze plastering in seconds to her bare thighs. "Those shoes aren't my size."

"The sneakers are for me."

Inch by inch, he glided his tongue along his bottom lip. "I prefer the heels that you're wearing."

"Good. Besides, the sneakers are only for my back-up plan."

"Back up?"

"Just in case, you run off. I'm going to kick off these heels, put on my sneakers, and race after you. I'm not going to let you run away this time."

"Trust me, when I say this. I won't be running anymore." He pierced her with his gaze. "You know the problem with that?"

"What?"

"I won't let you run away from me either."

"I'll never race away from a man that takes care of me."

He flashed her a wicked smile. "Never say never, Diana."

She opened her legs and exposed all of the lush, warm flesh in between her thighs. "I'll say whatever I want to."

"Interesting," he whispered in a hoarse voice. "And is that my shirt?"

Diana opened her mouth, but Asher didn't wait for her to say another damn thing as he rushed toward her. She shrieked, unprepared for him to launch her way.

"Asher, what are you—"

He picked her up before he could say anything else, and cradled her in his arms. "I swear I would take you right here if I didn't have half the staff on duty."

She nuzzled into his chest. His suit smelled fresh, like he'd just picked it up from the launderer. She ran her fingers through his damp hair.

He just took a shower? Did he do that just for me?

Asher carried her up the stairs and through the main hallway, until they ended up in his bedroom.

"Take the shirt off." Asher set her down on the floor and shut his door.

"What shirt?"

He lifted the ride side of his lip up into a sneer. "Don't

play with me, Diana."

"What happened to *my love*?"

"Take off your shirt, and I'll tell you what happened to my love."

Diana opened it, and let the shirt slide down her body.

"Fuck." He grabbed her waist, pushed her up against the door, and pressed his lips against hers.

"Jesus," she mumbled.

"You'll be calling for more than him by the end of the night." He wove his hands through her black curls and she gasped at the electric charge, at the power that came when his mouth moved against hers.

Diana panted beneath Asher's tender touch and rough kisses. "Asher?"

He hadn't heard her, he moved his hands to hers, held them up over her head against the door.

"Asher," she said louder.

He pulled back, his expression full of concern. "I'm sorry. What's wrong?"

She shook her head. "No, don't be. I just want to know why you're clothes are still on."

Asher smiled and it was enough to get Diana wet for him. She couldn't explain why something so simple as a grin from him made her want to do something crazy.

Asher stripped off his suit and shirt but he went at a snail's pace and Diana ached for his touch. His mouth on her skin. His dick inside of her.

She sauntered over to him and pushed his hands aside.

"Let me do it."

He arched his eyebrows. "You're bossy when you're—"

"Shut up, Asher." She placed kisses down his chest, until she reached the top of his slacks. Slowly, she left soft, wispy breaths on his flesh as she undid his button and unzipped him.

"Yes, definitely bossy."

"Not bossy, but I am a boss of some sorts." She wriggled the pants down his muscular legs. Those thighs bulged with strength, and she hoped, she'd get a chance to decorate that sexy flesh with her teeth. "Be careful, you don't want me to fire you, do you?"

"No," he said in a low voice. "I need this job."

She wanted to eat him, devour this man, until he was nothing but an empty shell that she could pass out by, and lay next to.

With her fingertips, she traced lines up his legs, thighs, and stopped short of his soft, plump sac. "Have you come to work, prepared, Mr. Bishop?"

"Yes, Mrs. Carson." She pulled his boxers down with her teeth.

Asher moaned.

She kneeled before him, his swollen cock hers for the taking. Her pussy dripped with desire. And Jesus did she want him. She reached around and stuck a manicured finger in his puckered asshole.

He groaned, "You're a naughty girl, Diana."

"No, I'm a boss." She grabbed the base of his dick with her other hand. Leaned down and took him into her mouth.

Her hair fanned out around her and between his moans, he brushed it out of her way.

"Let me show you what I'm talking about." Inch by hard inch, she licked up his shaft, sucked the tip, and rotated her hand around his dick while she took him even deep.

He tugged at her hair and gently pressed the back of her head, pushing her down a little bit more. A pleasure moan escaped her wet lips as she sucked down hard on his cock, taking it far into her throat, and wishing she could swallow it whole.

"Fuck. . ." He thrust into her, clenching his ass cheeks to feel every part of her mouth. "God, yes, you are a boss. My boss."

Diana wanted him to come, but she couldn't bear the thought of not having him release inside of her first. Shivering with lust, she pulled away from him and stood up. "Fuck me hard. Don't you want to be the employee of the month?"

Although a chuckle left his mouth, he did as he was told and pushed her to his bed. She fell back with a shriek, her full breasts bobbing from the reaction, her pussy throbbing to be filled, and every inch of her flesh vibrating with the call to be ravished.

He pinned her arms above her head. "Look at me."

She stared at him.

"I don't ever want you to turn away or close your eyes, when I fuck you."

She widened her gaze. "Okay."

"I want to see every second of what's going on in between those beautiful eyelids, I want to see my face in your eyes as you scream my fucking name." He pushed into her, hard.

It was thunderous thrust, more pleasure than pain.

She bit back a yelp, and almost turned away, before stopping herself.

He filled her so completely, right then. With every thrust, he brought her a little closer to the edge.

"I think I'm going to—"

He bit at her erect nipples. "No thinking. And you're not going to come yet. It's far too soon. I have so many things planned for us tonight."

Asher pulled out of her. Her desire dripped all over his length. He loved her wetness on him, relished in the slickness. "You're so wet. I wonder how you taste."

Falling to his knees, he brought his mouth to her wet pussy, parted those moist lips with his tongue, and lapped up her wetness. "Diana, you taste… amazing."

She arched her back and melted into him. She'd been fucked, sucked and made love to before, but she'd never felt the intensity of the moment as she did with Asher.

He delved his tongue further inside of her, touching the spot that made her toes curl and her hands grasp at the sheets.

As if Asher couldn't get enough desire from her, he took a finger, massaging her wetness from her cunt down to her asshole. He circled around the hole and she cried out.

"You like this, Diana? Do you want me to be naughty?"

She could barely form words together.

"Remember," he whispered. "You're the boss."

She just nodded and looked into his eyes as our whole body raged with lust.

"Yes, ma'm." He went back down, licking her inner thighs and moving over to her clit. The moment he sucked that throbbing bud into his mouth, she bucked up her hips and he slipped his finger into her hungry hole.

"Oh!" she moaned, overwhelmed with it all. Her appetite for Asher grew with every twitch of his tongue, and every flick of his finger. "I want you in me, Asher."

He brought his head up and shook it. "Not yet, my love. You're going to come in my mouth until your juices drip from my chin."

"Oh," was all she could mumble.

He thrust his finger in and out of her while his tongue searched for the part of her that would give him what he wanted. She was certain his tongue was a weapon of mass destruction, set on destroying her completely.

And good God was he doing it.

In and out.

Faster, then slower.

Harder and then soft,

So soft.

He bit at her clit and it was the proverbial foot on the grenade.

She gasped and an orgasm rock through her. "Asher. Oh God. I can't…"

Asher didn't stop though, he kept his tongue at the base of her cunt, lapping as she came in his mouth.

When her limbs turned to jelly and her muscles ached, only then did Asher remove his mouth from her, and without hesitation he pushed his cock inside of her.

"God, I've waited so long to feel this." He pulled out slowly, thrust in harder, and repeated over and over again.

"Now you've done it." He grasped at Diana's breasts, so full and voluptuous. "Now I won't let you go."

He fucked her hard, triggering a staccato of moans to push out of her and echo through the room. "Oh! Oh! Oh! Oh!"

But, he still he wasn't ready to finish, he pulled out and flipped her over.

She was barely able to take another breath before, he thrust inside of her from behind. And when he entered her that time, it nearly undid her. She could've let it all go there, but she held on for Asher.

She wanted to come again, but with him, together.

"Harder. I want to feel you in my stomach," she screeched.

Her words seemed to set him on fire and he did what she asked. He moved so fast, his balls slapped against her ass and she reveled in the sound.

Her moans were pings of one word that spit out of her opened mouth with no control. "Oh! Oh! Oh! Oh!"

That was all she had to say, all that she could form her lips to moan. "Oh! Oh!Oh! Oh!"

His cock sent her into overdrive. An intense numbness started at her toes, she was so close to being shoved over the edge for the second time, and hoped to God that he was close, cause she had nothing else left in her.

"Oh. Oh. Oh. Oh."

"God Diana, you're…" He didn't finish his sentence but with three harder, deep thrusts he finished in her. Their moans intermingled into one long sound, and he panted.

Diana's heart raced and she felt weightless, like she could float right up to the clouds. Unlike every man she'd been with before, Asher didn't immediately remove himself from her body. He traced circles into the flesh of her back. It sent shivers through her.

He stayed in her, though she didn't know why.

She liked it.

It was intimate.

Sexy.

Like he didn't need to disengage from her. It made her feel like he wanted her, even after his dick was done.

He kissed her down the spine. "You're the boss."

She laughed in a hoarse, after-sex way. "You're obligated to say that when you're dick is still inside of me."

"No. I mean it."

"They all do," she whispered.

"I'm not all men."

"Maybe, you're not."

He pulled out of Diana, turned her over, grasped her jaw, and brought that lovely face close to him. "I'm not like any man you've ever known. I'm your favorite nightmare and your worst dream all in one. I'm everything you shouldn't want. And you're everything I need. Everything I don't deserve."

She swallowed though her throat was scratchy and raw. He spoke with such confidence. And although, she believed him, she needed a moment to recoup.

"Coffee," she blurted out.

Shock fell over his face. "Huh?"

"I need coffee," she said.

He brushed her black curls away and kissed her forehead. "You want coffee?"

"Yes."

"Okay." He kissed her forehead, and it reminded her of how Neil would do it long ago, when they first got married. If Diana hadn't missed that part of marriage so much, she might've been creeped out. But it felt right with Asher. Everything did.

And that scared her.

"Oh, I need to tell you something," Asher said. "There was another murder tonight. I heard it on the police scanner on the way home from the office."

Diana sat up straight. "What? Why didn't you tell me earlier?"

"And miss out on the chance to fuck you senseless? No thanks. It didn't feel like the right time." Asher climbed out of the bed. Moonlight seeped in from the window and hit his skin. The layers of muscle on his back flexed as he stretched.

God, he's a thing of beauty.

He turned back to her. "I just wanted you to know, because I think you forget this creep is still out there. Still killing."

Diana shook her head. "Jesus. I have to get to the office. I need to get a jump on this story."

"No, you need to stay right here for the night where it's safe. Tomorrow, in the daylight, you can investigate to your heart's content."

She loathed being treated like a fragile child. Like a woman who didn't know the dangers facing her. But if everything went according to plan, she'd have Cupid in her sights soon enough.

She gave up, and relaxed in that warm bed of his, relishing in his scent as it clung to the sheets. "Yeah, I guess you're right."

He kissed her on the forehead. "Of course I am."

Asher left Diana naked and trembling in her post-sex nerves.

Wait a minute. He didn't even put any clothes on, before leaving his bedroom and running downstairs.

She was sure his staff had seen him naked plenty of times, he probably was not the type of man to care, but Diana wasn't that comfortable yet.

I'll grab one of his shirts and put it on, since he clearly won't be using any.

She climbed out of his immaculate bed and stalked toward the closet.

What does a man like Asher Bishop have in his closet?

She opened the door and stuck her head in. It was an enormous space, one that would make any shopping freak orgasm. There was a walk way in the center that stretched out at least severn to ten feet. Shelves of shoes, hooks with ties, and clear compartments for other accessories sat on the right. Hanging clothes stood on the right, full of everything any well-dressed man could imagine—designer suits, high-brand sportswear, expensive casual items, and more and more.

In the middle, there was a little string that she pulled. It cast an orangey glow into the spacious area.

Rows and rows of suits in various shades of black and gray and navy hung meticulously. Freshly pressed shirts all in color coordinated waves. She fingered the fabric as she moved to the end of the closet.

A long mirror hung on the back of the wall. But something was odd, instead of it remaining stuck all the way to the wall. There was a gap, as if the mirror served more as a door to a compartment.

And that's where I bet, Mr. Bishop keeps all of his porn. Hmmmm. What type of naughty things do you hide in your closet?

Walking all the way to the back, she clasped her hands on the edge of the mirror and pulled it back. A black curtain hung behind it. She parted the thick, velvet fabric away. Confusion caught her first, than curiosity.

What is that?

Thin metal poles hung in front of her. She dragged her

gaze down to their bottoms, and gasped when she spotted their sharpened tips. They sparkled in the closet's dim lightening.

Arrows. No. Fuck. No. Those are not arrows.

Fear pumped through her veins. A booming sounded in her ears. She glanced back, real quick, and strained to hear if Asher was coming.

Arrows. Those are arrows. Why are those arrows. Fuck.

She shook, so hard her teeth chattered. Her curiosity bit at her and she touched one and then pulled back, the sharp edge tearing at her flesh. Blood pooled at the tiny wound and droplets landed on the white carpet by her feet.

No. God, please no.

She was all alone, in the back of Asher's closet, and he kept arrows there. Checking behind her once again, she risked a further look, lifted her shivering fingers, pushed away the arrows, and touched the dark object laying behind them.

A polished, steel bow.

Next to it sat a bag of arrows, the silver tips sparkling.

No… this can't be.

Something compelled her to look away, though she wanted to memorize every inch of what she was seeing, in case she was dreaming. But her eyes gravitated toward something else that hung on a tiny shelf above the arrows.

Black gloves.

No, no, no. This is all wrong.

Asher's whistling sounded behind her, his footsteps came

next.

Fuck.

In a rush, she pushed the mirror back, stumbled to the light's rope, pulled it, rushed out of the now dark closet, and breathed hard in and out, as she raced over to the bed.

He has a bow and arrows.

His whistling came closer. He rounded the corner, right before she could get back in the bed. For some reason, she froze right there with her mouth open, unable to say anything.

Why would he have the gloves? I know why.

God, I know why.

CHAPTER SEVENTEEN

CUPID

"Is everything okay?" Asher asked.

"Y-yes. Of course. Why wouldn't I be? I'm just fine." She cleared her throat.

They stood there, and stared at each other.

"What were you doing?" Asher asked.

"What do you mean?"

"Your naked and standing next to the bed."

"You're naked with a tray of coffee and standing next to the doorway."

"Okay," he said.

What's wrong?

"Umm. So. . ." She rushed past him. "I'll be right back."

"Where are you going?" He turned around and did his best to not rattle the tray holding both of their cups of coffee.

He'd requested something special from Grace who, for some reason, was beyond ecstatic with Diana staying at the house. She'd even given him an array of delights to take back to her. Along with the two cups of coffee, there were several spices and flavorings. Tiny cups of cinnamon, brown sugar, honey, and caramel. Cubes of chocolate rested on one plate. Tiny pastries and globes of melon sat on another.

A blood red rose lay right at the top of the tray.

"Diana?" Asher called louder as she continued out of the bedroom. "Diana!"

"Yes?" She paused in the doorway and slowly glanced over her shoulder.

"Where are you going?"

"I. . .just thought that I should clean up in my room."

"Why?" he asked.

"Why not?" She took a step out of the doorway.

The movement caught him off guard. He wrinkled his forehead.

Something is different. Or is it just me? She did just lose her husband. Maybe, she feels weird or even worse. . .guilty. Does she still consider herself married? Is this adultery to her? I wish I could kill Neil again.

"I'll be right back." She headed away.

"Wait."

She stopped and slowly turned around again, laying her hands to the side and clenching her fingers in and out.

What's going on?

He glanced down at her feet. Instead of in a relaxed position, she kept them in a guarded stance—far apart with the heel up on the foot that was closest to me.

It had to be his mind playing tricks on him in some way, because she looked like she was ready to attack.

Something is wrong. What changed? Did I do something? Is it me or Neil's ghost?

"Relax." He backed up to the dresser, set the tray on top, picked up the rose, and brought it to her. "I just wanted to give you this."

Diana didn't even look down at the flower. Instead, she stared at his face, as if she was gazing at him for the first time.

Why is she looking at me like that? Was the sex that good...or that bad?

Asher held the rose in front of her.

Yet, still, she just stared at him.

"Diana?"

"What?" She blinked and edged back. "I'm sorry. What did you say?"

"Do you not like roses?" He gestured to the one in his hand.

"I do." She kept her hands to her sides. "I'll enjoy that beautiful...gift, after my shower." She inched back some more. "Okay?"

He twisted the rose's stem in his fingers. "Okay."

She walked away, and he watched her every shivering step. Counting each time her foot shook as it hit the ground.

He'd seen many scared women walk away from him. Every time he let a girl go before he killed the man that she was unlucky to be harmed by.

They'd all rushed off on quivering feet.

Just like Diana did in that very moment.

Even his mother had started walking away from him in the same manner. It was after the third husband. She became afraid of him, her own son. After the third husband, even she had had that same rush in her steps, in the times that she feared him.

I don't know what's going on, but things will not change, Diana. Whether it's Neil's ghost or something to do with me, you will be mine for as long as I need you to be.

"Diana!"

She jumped and twisted around, edging back a little and never truly stopping her path away from him. "Y-yes."

He forced himself to smile at her. "Have a good shower."

Diana widened her eyes. "Thanks."

She said nothing else, turned back around, and picked up her pace.

Interesting. She's terrified. Why?

Darkness swarmed in his chest, but he pushed it at bay. There was no need to worry too much with her. They'd made love.

But he could smell her panic in the air.

Something else has to be going on.

This was why he didn't deal with women too much. They were all so complex, each one with their own puzzle and convoluted clues. Before Diana, no women's brain-teasing confusions had been worth him solving. He played their games for a night or two, and then went about his way.

Diana was different.

He'd spend the rest of his life, piecing together every inch of her.

Let's see if I can do my own investigation on Miss Prized Reporter.

She slammed the door behind her, and he walked off to the staircase and headed down to the first floor.

The rose remained in his hand, as he hurried to his closet, put on some pants, and headed to his hidden security room.

It took him no time to get there. Most didn't know it existed, only the house manager and head of security. Neither had the code for the door, and both needed permission to ever review a necessary tape. Too many things occurred in his house, and by his hand. Half of the time, he kept the recording for his own records.

He got to the black, metal door and pressed in his mother's birthday.

A beep sounded, and then a click. The door opened, and he headed in, right as it closed behind him.

Should I even do this? Maybe, I am just a little off. Our minds are the creators of our reality. Diana's anxiety could all be in my head.

Disruptive thoughts plagued his mind.

Eight TV screens stood in front of him. Each one displayed a different part of his property for ten seconds and then shifted to another camera. Every room had a mini-camera in the ceiling. Even more devices were nailed in the trees all over the grounds.

No one would come or leave without him knowing it.

Asher turned on the left control panel, switched the monitor next to him to *operator*. In this mode, he could focus on one camera's recordings, focus in on the person in the room, or pull back. Additionally, he could rewind and play what had already been recorded.

He found his bedroom's camera and rewound the recording back to several minutes ago.

On the screen, Diana and he lay on the bed, their bodies entangled against each other as they moved together in perfect rhythm. Lust soared to his groin.

God, what am I doing? I should be running run up there and taking Diana in the shower.

Her pussy had been heaven. There was no other way for him to say it. No matter how much heavenly words one used to describe that flesh between her legs, none could compare to the raw truth.

Her pussy had been heaven, and he would've been happy to die right there between those moist lips.

He rubbed his face with both of his hands and sighed. "Focus, Asher."

He pressed the fast forward button to where he'd left Diana by herself. "This is stupid. I should be upstairs in the shower with her, but here I am, being. . .me."

On the screen, a devilish grin spread across Diana's face as she got up from the bed and walked toward her closet.

He quirked an eyebrow. "What was on your mind, Diana?"

She stepped in and scanned the area.

You're such a curious cat. I'm not liking where this is going, Diana.

The closet's light turned on and bathed her in light. All he could see was her back as she continued to enter, moving her head from side to side as she probably took in the massive space.

Dread hit Asher's gut. No one ever went in his closet. Not even his staff.

It was another odd thing about him.

I forgot to tell her not to go in my closet.

All his life, the closet had been a safe haven. When his father beat his mother to a pulp, he would run in there, keeping all of his secret items in the little space, for when he would need to run away and get help. That was the crazy things that went through his little, innocent mind, as terror rained down around him.

Young Asher had kept a plastic Indian bow and arrow in his closet, just for the occasion to hurt his father.

He'd even used it one night.

At dinner, his father snatched his mother up by her neck and slung the weak woman into the table. Everything crashed around them—dinner fell to the floor. Plates smashed into bits and pieces. Peas and mashed potatoes got all over Asher's sneakers.

"No!" With his tiny feet, he'd ran to his closet, grabbed the brown and green bow, picked up the orange arrows, rushed back to his dad, pulled the bow back, and let go.

The arrow shot through the air, barely poked at his father's back, and then dropped to the floor.

"Ash Tray, was that you?" His father stopped punching his mother in the face and turned to him. "Ash Tray? Get your ass out of here, before I come for you."

Running away, Asher dropped the bow and arrow, ignored the closet, and got back to his other hiding spot under his bed.

Back in reality, Asher pushed that old memory away and watched Diana on the screen as she walked all the way to the back of the closet, flipped back the mirror, and reached her hands inside his secret compartment.

Great job. I go through all the trouble for so many years to be careful, and not get caught, and here I let a prized investigating reporter stumble into my closet right where all of my secrets are.

Asher couldn't see what she was touching, but he knew. He'd been in that closet day after day, gazing at his bow and arrow. He no longer was forced to deal with the plastic toys of his youth. Now he had a real one—high definition and worth more money than an average American's car.

From now on, when he pulled his bow back, his target was hit, and there would be no more hurt by any bad man.

"Diana. Diana," Asher whispered as he stared at the screen.

Even in the recording, he could see the fear in her eyes as she rushed out of there. He checked the night stand where her phone still sat.

Good. She's just focusing on getting herself out of here. I don't think she ever grabbed her phone. It definitely wasn't in her hand when she went to the shower.

He put his hand into his pocket, took out his phone, and dialed security.

One of his guards answered, "Hello, Mr. Bishop."

"How are you doing, Dwight?" Asher asked.

"Very good, sir."

"I'm having a bit of an uncomfortable situation. Nothing that we really need to worry about in reference to the security of this property, but my guest, Mrs. Carson, however, has taken something that has sort of. . .how do I say this without being inappropriate? Hmm. This substance has altered her mind."

"Okay. I understand."

"So I don't know if you are used to dealing with people who take . . . mind-altering substances, but it can be a bit crazy."

Dwight chuckled. "In this line of security work, especially on Ovid Island, I've dealt with a lot of situations where people have used these substances."

"Good." Asher smiled. "Mrs. Diane Carson has taken something. I'm trying to keep her calm. She's going to take a shower and eat, but there might be a point where the paranoia continues. She may even want to leave the property and try driving a car. We can't have that."

"No, sir."

"I care about this woman. You know there's been no other

woman besides my mother that's been able to walk these hallways overnight."

"Yes, sir. The staff have been talking about it all week."

That made Asher uneasy, but he decided to deal with that later. There were too many other things going on.

Deal with it all, one by one. There's only a threat, if I don't handle it. I can handle Diana. I just need time.

"Good," Asher said. "I'm glad I'll have help with keeping Mrs. Carson on the property until she comes down from this crazy trip she's having."

"No problem, sir. You have a good evening."

"You too." Asher hung up the phone and left the security room.

CHAPTER EIGHTEEN

CUPID

An hour later, footsteps sounded on the stairs. On the first level of his mansion, Asher stood in the shadows, in an area close to the bottom of the steps.

The whole time, he held onto the rose, he'd wanted to give to Diana.

There you go. Now it's time to escape from the bad man.

He'd been waiting for her to run, and figured the front or back door would be her only rational solution. The windows were hard to climb out of. He'd done it a few times, constantly scraping himself and pulling a muscle.

For Diana, climbing down three flights on his mansion, would be suicide.

I'm guessing Diana no longer is interested in taking a shower. You figured now was a good time to run away?

In front of him, Diana walked down the steps. She glanced behind her, every few feet, probably assuming that

Asher still lay in his bedroom.

What's going through your mind? Are you scared?

He relished in the hallway's darkness, leaned back, and let the shade blanket him.

Do you know I'm Cupid? Or are there doubts? Do you think I'm capable of murder, My Love?

Diana arrived at the first floor, hugged herself, and headed toward his direction. He'd guessed right. Diana hadn't remembered the back exits, when he'd done his tour of the house.

Now. How do I talk to her, without scaring her.

Diana's heavy breathing sounded out as she sped-walked toward him, not having any idea he was there.

Poor Diana.

Hope glittered in her eyes. Could she see the door in her mind? Did she imagine herself placing her hands on the knob, turning it, and running away from him?

No. Boy meets girl. Boy falls in love. The girl too. And then they have a small spat, nothing more. But. . .girl does not flee from the boy in fear. Not his girl.

"Okay, Diana," she whispered to herself.

She was only five feet away, and would past him in seconds. She'd only need several more feet to hit the door. Although, unbeknownst to her, none of that mattered. His security would keep her here.

Tonight, Diana was trapped.

Tomorrow, he'd think of another way, to keep her in his cage.

Love truly is difficult.

"Y-you've got it." Diana picked up her pace and formed her fingers into fists. "Almost there."

"Almost where?" Asher flipped the hallway's switch. A bright lamp lit up the hallway.

Gasping, Diana stared at him and didn't move.

Smart. It's best to say nothing. Focus on the escape. Don't show too much fear. Trick me. Make me believe you're still here for me.

She relaxed her arms as best as she could and held her hands, twisting each finger a little. "Asher? Did you forget something?"

"No." He turned the rose around. Those petals glowed in the light as they spiraled down over and over around the thorny stem. "Where were you going, Diana?"

"I went to the bedroom, but you weren't in there."

Good save, Diana. This is why I like you. You're so smart.

"Sorry, I left. I was wondering about something." He raised the rose in the light. "I just had to check it out, and now I know."

"Know what?"

"I'm not sure."

"Then you don't know."

"Maybe, you're right." He turned the rose around again. "Maybe, I don't know."

A few silent seconds passed. The whole time Asher studied the flower.

Diana wiped the sweat off of her forehead and gave him a

weak smile. "That is such a captivating rose."

"It is." He gazed at Diana and with his hands, pulled away one petal. "She loves me?"

The crimson petal floated down to the floor. It reminded him of the first drop of blood in a kill. That was always his favorite part, anytime his arrow hit a target.

That first drop of blood was like a flame to a cigarette or the addict's act of lighting a spoon and sucking up the bubbling liquid with a rusty needle.

The first drop of blood triggered the beginning of the fun, the start of all the madness.

Asher gazed at the petal as it lay on the floor between Diana and him.

In some ways, this petal is like the first drop of blood for our relationship. But let's see, if I'll have to shed more blood in the days to come. What will I do with you, Sweet Diana?

"She loves me not?" He snapped another petal off and flung it in the air.

Diana backed up. "Is. . .is everything okay?"

He formed his lips to a grim line. "Do you know where that came from?"

"Where what came from?" She made a fist with one hand and put it behind her.

"That whole little phrase." He picked a petal. "She loves me?"

He snatched another and flung it in the air. "She loves me not?"

"Do I know where, *she loves me, she loves me not* came

from?"

"Yeah."

"No." She shook her head. "I have no idea."

"It was a French game. A curious boy would pick a petal off a flower for each phrase." Asher stalked toward her in a slow motion, almost like a wolf would creep toward an innocent doe as it lapped at a stream. "The object of his affection represented the flower. The phrase is repeated until all of the petals are discarded.

"I've played the game." She tensed as he stopped right in front of her.

"The final petal is plucked and represents the true statement of whether the object of his affection really loves him or not."

"Do you believe that?" he asked with barely a foot of distance between them.

Her bottom lip quivered. "What?"

"Do you believe that the flower could predict the truth of a man's love?"

"No. Why would I?"

Step by step, he circled her. It was wrong of him. He knew how scared she was, but he couldn't help it. The terror radiating from her skin made him even more hungrier for her.

It was wrong, but his dick grew hard in his pants as she tensed her shoulders up.

He walked around her again, that time, talking to her with each step. "Flowers are believed to have this symbolic tie to humanity. Roses have always been connected with love.

They've been known to phrophesize great things."

"What do you think this rose would say about us?" He got right in front of her, his bare chest touching her shaking one.

But something odd happened with their closeness.

She didn't step back, and her shivering decreased to almost nothing.

Within the quiet, she breathed in and out, then stared up at him. "I don't know what that rose would say about us."

"No?" He inhaled the lushness of her fragrance.

Was he angry that she found the bow and arrow? No. Scared a little. Determined to keep her around. Maybe even a bit tinkering off into the dark side of how much he'd planned to keep her near him.

But he wasn't angry.

He wouldn't hurt her.

Keep her?

Yes.

Somehow.

But he wouldn't hurt her,

Or he would do his best.

Did she realize that same truth in that moment? Or was she simply trying to calm herself down?

She lifted her chin and gazed at him. "I don't think our love would be represented by a regular rose."

"No?"

She turned around and headed back up the stairs. "No. Our love started with blood. Wouldn't you say?"

What's your plan now, Diana? And how do I stop you?

How do I show you that I'm not as bad?

He didn't move. She headed upstairs.

For now, there would be no need to worry about her leaving the house.

"Blood?" he asked.

"Yes." She paused on the stairs and stared down at him. "Our love. . .or really. . .whatever we have. It started with blood."

"Neil's blood?"

She flinched. "Yes."

"I'm sorry. I always forget that you're mourning."

"I am, and I'm not." She went up another stair and stopped.

"Maybe, that's a good thing."

"Maybe."

"But I'm wondering something." She targeted him with her gaze. "Why do you think Cupid picked Neil?"

Asher grinned. "How would I know?"

"I'm just wondering what your opinion is."

"I only know the few things that I heard about Neil. I'm not sure what Cupid found out, but I'm sure Cupid probably figured that Neil didn't deserve you, that this beast of a man was sticking his dick in every female on the island, and not even using any protection. Cupid probably guessed that no woman had earned the right to receive a lifetime of sexually transmitted diseases or even worse, AIDS from her own husband. A man that was supposed to protect and love his woman."

She gripped the rail on the staircase as if she was about to lose the strength in her legs. "Do you think Cupid knew that I was Neil's wife? Do you think Cupid saw me before he killed Neil?"

Asher let his gaze travel down to the curve of her hips that pressed against her jeans, and then he drank in those supple breasts that were tucked under her shirt. She'd dressed fast, but not fast enough.

He licked his lips. "No. I'm sure Cupid had never seen you. If he had, he might not have ever remembered to kill Neil or his mistress."

She widened her eyes, but terror didn't linger in them. Asher couldn't confirm that it was lust, but it was better than the terror.

She touched her chest. "You want me to stay here, because you think Cupid wants to kill me?"

"No." He tucked the rose behind one ear. "I want you to stay here, because I can't think of any other woman or person I want to have next to me every night."

"Tonight was only a one-time thing."

"I believe you're mistaken."

"What do you think Cupid would believe?" she asked.

Careful, Diana. You're not ready to meet the monster yet. Maybe, you should only focus on Asher for tonight.

"Cupid doesn't deal with love," he said.

"No?" Diana asked. "Then what do you think Cupid deals with?"

"Death. Just death."

"Are you sure?"

"As much as I could be, Diana."

"That's a shame," she said as she continued up the stairs. "I'm tired. I should go to sleep. . .in my own room. I'm so sorry, but I'm out of it. Besides, I have more interviews with Cupid's victims' tomorrow morning. Remember?" She kept her back to me. "And then there's possibly a new victim."

"Yes." Asher thought back then to the bloody scene and message to Diana that he'd left behind.

"Fuck." He cringed.

"Did you say anything?" Diana called back from the top of the stairs.

"No. Goodnight."

The bloody message to Diana flashed in his head. Earlier, he'd put wrote the blood on the wall to scare her into staying at the house longer. Cupid was supposed to be some crazy guy that could be stalking her. It was just supposed to be this quick fix to buy him some more days.

But now Diana knew that he was Cupid.

How could she not?

A bow and arrow lay in his closet. And he, himself, had shown a huge interest into the Cupid murders, even funding her with a lot of money to investigate it.

How stupid had he been to think he could keep his identity a secret from Diana?

Tomorrow, she would either go to the scene herself or be told by the police. They'd have to connect her as the Diana in the message. It would make sense to at least check with the fifth's victim's widow who happened to also be named Diana.

He didn't worry about Diana telling the cops about him. What proof would she have? The bow and arrow would be gone from the closet, as well as anything else on his property.

Asher also had a strong alibi for Neil's murder, over two hundred partying guests would confirm that he was there. He even had an alibi for this recent murder. He always maintained footage of him sitting in the office at different parts of a given day. It would take no time to slip a pre-recorded disk out and have the security hand that to the police.

The cops would see him in his office all evening just like he said he'd been.

If anything, they would think Diana was crazy, and getting that label on small, yet wealthy Ovid Island, would further cage her to him.

She'll have nowhere to escape, not until I'm done.

He returned to the bloody message he'd left her earlier.

"Damn it." He ran his fingers through his blonde curls.

She knows I'm Cupid, and now I've written her name in fucking blood on a door above a dead body. Even worse, I carved the damn name she gave me into his chest.

He blew out a long breath.

Fucking fantastic! Now she's going to see the message and think I'm crazy!

"You are crazy," his mother said behind him.

Shocked, he twisted around and yanked the rose from his ear. "Mom, what are you doing here?"

"Saving your ass as usual." She fanned herself, took off the leather jacket she always wore, and captured him in her arms. "She won't find out about you, Baby. I'll make sure of it."

"No." He pushed her away. "No, I don't need your help. I want you to go back to Paris."

"But, darling—"

"No." He pushed at her again. "I don't need you this time."

"No?" Her image rippled in front of him. "Are you sure, Honey?"

His chest filled with fear, but he nodded. "I'm sure."

And in the next moment, his mother evaporated in front of him.

He stood there for a long time. Moments like that were hard for him to swallow. It was in those seconds when he realized that his mother was actually dead.

He didn't like those times.

Yes. That's right.

He released another long breath.

I killed Mother. I really have to stop forgetting that.

CHAPTER NINETEEN

DIANA

Diana paced back and forth in the bedroom she no longer felt comfortable in. Thoughts bounced around her skull like a pinball machine.

She'd slept with Asher.

And, Asher was Cupid.

Jesus!

Cupid was Asher.

And he'd killed Neil.

She didn't think about Neil's young life being taken from him by a bow and arrow. Neither did she give any thoughts to his dead mistress. Instead, she shook with fury that the hunt was over.

She'd barely gotten started. The ache to discover Cupid's identity had burrowed so deep inside of her, and it had been ripped right from her grasp.

By accident.

Why had she snooped? Why couldn't she have just laid in

bed with post-sex bliss dripping from her dark, velvet skin? She would have been none the wiser and the thrill—that itch to do what she did best would still be there.

I'm going crazy. I just slept with the man that killed my husband, and I'm irritated that I found it out so soon. I should just escape away from him, and run right into a mental hospital.

What was she to do? She was certain Asher sensed the change in her. He'd given her a strange look, almost as if he could smell Diana's mingling emotions emanating from her flesh.

She wasn't as scared as she should have been. Perhaps it was because Cupid's kills had always held meaning.

There was reason behind the murders.

Logical, decipherable justifications.

Diana truly believed, even after knowing the truth, that Cupid didn't want her dead.

It wasn't that she was scared of Cupid—it was more that she was terrified she had developed feelings for him.

She respected him.

Honored his code.

Anyone who killed a man that raped his daughter nightly, was no enemy of mine, but. . .what do I do? Too much has happened. This man kills people. He's a psychopath or sociopath, or freaking both. I don't know.

She'd held Asher in her arms. Kissed his lips in a hundred different ways. Seen the way his blonde curls fell over his eyes when he bent down to suck on her nipples.

Her visions of Asher and Cupid swirled together, until she couldn't decipher who was who and how she felt about them separately. They were one in the same and the more she thought about it—the more anxious she became.

There was a part of Diana that wanted to expose him to the Ovid Island residents, for the sheer fact that he thought he could hide it. But there were other parts of her that dulled the rash decisions.

She wanted to ask him a hundred questions.

Had she always been part of his plan? How many more men had died at his hand? Why was he this way?

But how? How do you ask a man you've embraced and exchanged kisses with why he kills, as if it's a completely natural question?

Had her cell phone not gone off, she would have spent hours circling the endless cycle of questions she wanted to know.

"Hello?"

"Diana, it's Greg. There's been another murder."

Diana swallowed and for a brief second, she believed she made the entire night up in her head. If Cupid killed again, surely he would have been dealing with his mess. Not wrapped up in his lover's arms.

"Where?"

"South Manhatten Avenue."

"Are you sure it's related to the Cupid murders? That's below his comfort level for rich men."

Her boss sighed. "I'm sure. Look, you just... really

should get down here. There's something you need to see for yourself."

Diana's heart raced. She'd was usually kept *out* of the crime scenes, not summoned to them. "Right. Okay, I'll be there as soon as I can."

She hugged the phone to her chest after her boss hung up. She stayed very still and tried to detect the anxiety inside of her. The fear that should have course through her.

But Diana wasn't afraid. She was thrilled. She would pretend the hunt was still on. If only for the night, so she could revel in the vibrations of discovery and uncovering. Tomorrow, she would decide what to do. But that night, she would feign ignorance.

She threw on jeans and a t-shirt, pulled her black curls into a loose ponytail and rushed down the giant staircase.

"Asher!"

His name echoed through the giant space and there was no trace of movement.

"Asher?" She called out, more of a question than a demand.

Again, only darkness and silence answered her back.

"Oh this is ridiculous. Who needs a house this big anyway?" She mused aloud, rushing through the main hallway to the kitchen.

His chef jumped when Diana swung the door open.

"I'm sorry. I didn't mean to scare you. I'm looking for Asher. He's not… well, to be honest, I don't know where he's at in this house."

The woman was older, her eyes defined by the deep crows feet around them. Her gray hair slicked back in a bun only gave her a slightly professional edge, though her face reminded Diana of a grandmother's. Sweet, docile, forgiving. Did she have any idea what Asher was doing?

No, probably not. He had hidden it well. Her discovery was a mistake she wasn't meant to find.

"Oh Ma'am, that's a complex question. Asher is a... complex man. He likes to be everywhere all the time. Would you like me to get him for you?"

Diana nodded. "That would be lovely. Thank you."

The chef walked a few steps to a grey metal box against the wall. Pushed a few buttons and leaned into it.

"Mr. Bishop? You busy?"

For a few seconds, there was only silence. And then the machine crackled and Asher's voice filtered through the speaker. "What do you want Grace? Mother and I are having an important conversation."

Grace turned to look at Diana, her brows knitted together, a frown on her face. Diana looked back at Grace, confusion rising up inside of her.

Mother? Was he being facetious? Sarcastic? Why would he want his chef to think he was talking to his dead mother?

Grace sighed and spoke into the box again. "Sir, your guest is requesting your presence. She's come down to the kitchen looking for you."

"Dammit, Grace. Why didn't you just tell me this to begin with?" his voice was angry, but still controlled.

"I'm sorry, sir. What would you like me to tell her?"

The speaker crackled again. "I'll be down in a minute."

Grace turned around slowly, her mouth opened and closed, as if she wanted to say something but couldn't form the words.

"Does he do that often?" Diana asked her.

"Ma'am?"

"Say things about his mother. As if he's with her?"

Grace's gaze met Diana's. "I don't think it's my place…"

"You're worried about him, aren't you?"

It was barely perceptible, but Diana noticed the way Grace teared up. "Yes, Ma'am."

"How long has it been since Miss Bishop passed?"

"Seven years, Ma'am."

Diana stepped forward. "And he's been talking to her ever since?"

Grace nodded.

"You're a good woman, Grace," Diana said. "Let's pretend we didn't talk about this."

"Thank you Ma'am," Grace said in a whisper.

The door flung open and Asher stood there in a grey suit, his blond curls disheveled, his expression sour.

"Diana."

"Asher—"

Asher grabbed her wrist. "Come. Let's let Grace finish her kitchen duties. Thank you, Grace, for alerting me to Miss Carson's request."

Grace nodded and met Diana's gaze before Asher pulled

her through the door.

"I thought you were tired," Asher asked as he guided her to the sitting room.

"I was. But I just got a call."

"From whom?"

"My boss. There's been a murder and I need to get to the scene immediately," Diana said, using all of her strength to remain calm and in control. She forced herself to look him in the eye.

"Are you sure that's such a good idea? What if he's waiting for you to arrive."

Diana shrugged. "Then I would like to meet him. Ask him a few questions."

She expected Asher to be stunned but instead he chuckled. "Only you would want to meet the madman going around killing people. You should be terrified of him. Whatever would you ask?"

She didn't want to give herself away quite yet. She wanted to be sure of how she felt when she revealed what she knew. Her life might depend on it.

"The usual things. Motivation. Remorse. Those types of things."

"Is that all? You're not the least bit curious of anything else."

Diana smiled, nervously. "Of course I am. But this is all hypothetical. And I haven't got time for that. I need to go to a crime scene, remember?"

Asher nodded. "Yes, how could I forget. I'll get my driver

to take you."

"How about you come with me? It's your money at work after all. Nothing like seeing how it's being used, firsthand."

Asher shook his head. "That's not necessary. I believe you're doing a fine job. Besides… I have work tomorrow."

Diana walked toward the door. "It wasn't a question, Asher. You're coming with me."

Chapter Twenty

DIANA

Thirty minutes later, Diana and Asher stared out of opposing windows in the limo.

The silence between them grew like a tumor. She hadn't been sure if she would actually get Asher to come with her, but she was certain that once he was there, everything would become clearer.

She studied him as much as she could from the corner of her eye.

Okay. He kills people. The two scariest types of murderers are psychopaths and sociopaths. Which one are you, Asher? And how am I involved in your future?

She could go to the police, but she'd already ran that down in her head several times. He had the money and resources to cover it all up, or run off never to be found again, yet hidden in the shadows to take her life, whenever he craved her death.

She'd have to be careful, either way.

Every step in these next few days would have to be well-planned in order to trap him.

Asher turned her way. "I would like you to stay for two weeks, at least."

She tensed.

Of course you want me to stay. Had you planned on having me leave at all? If I stayed would it make me safer? The staff is all around. Everyone knows I'm in his mansion. If something happens to me, Asher would be the first person suspected. Right? God, I hope I'm right. But just in case, I'll fight it. Let's see what happens if I say no.

She swallowed down her fear. "No."

Shock laced his words. "No?"

"You sound surprised."

He hid his face into the shadows of the limo. "I am."

"That doesn't mean that I'm done with Cupid. We can still work on that part."

"Well, thank God for Cupid."

"I'm sorry, but I told you that we couldn't. . .have sex anymore."

He got back into the moonlight, as the limo made it down Poet Lane. Pain creased around the corners of his eyes. "You're done with me?"

"I-I'm. . ."

"Let me guess for you." He spat out the words. "You're mourning? Confused? Worried? Nervous?" He waited for a few seconds, and then just said it, "Scared?"

"Maybe."

"Maybe," he muttered and went back to looking out of his side of the limo window. "Let me explain something to you, Mrs. Carson."

She smirked. "We're back at Mrs. Carson?"

He ignored the smart ass comment. "I'm glad you're not done with Cupid." His voice came out darker than ever before. "However, I'm certainly not done with you, either."

"That's too bad. I'll have to disappoint you, if you try to make a move on me. The sex was a mistake."

"No, Diana." He turned to her and pierced her with a heated gaze. "The sex was only the beginning."

Has he lost his mind? Uh. . .yes. He's a freaking serial killer. He lost his mind long ago. He talks about his mother like she really exists. Why am I in this limo with him again?

She bit her lip and stared in front of her.

A quiet settled upon them as the limo sluggishly rolled through Ovid Island.

Hurry. I got to get out of this car. It's getting hard to breath, and I don't know if it's fear or lust that's coursing through my veins.

Even though a decent amount of space sat between them. His warmth radiated from his body and caressed her. She yearned to run her fingers through those blonde curls that she'd played with while they made love. Her tongue craved a lick of his skin and a wrestle with his tongue. Her teeth ached to bite the curve of his neck, and just taste him for one more time.

No. Get that out of your head right now. No. Damn it,

driver. Hurry.

Diana was sure the vehicle drove at a regular speed and that it was more her impatience of wanting to see what Greg had summoned her to rather than her desire to escape his presence. Sex with Asher would not be something that she even allowed to play upon her mind. She would *not* think about his dick or the way it felt in her hands. In her mouth. Inside of her.

No, no, no.

Yet, the memory of his tongue's sensations on her body, rocked her, right in that moment. A low moan fled her lips, before she could even stifle it.

And he had to have heard her, because he turned to her and raised the right side of his lip into a sneer, as if he was just as hungry for her, and just as mad about it.

Her face flushed like she'd been running. That was what he did to her, with just one night of sex, had her thinking about the things he did to her flesh, whether she wanted to or not.

And his cock,
so thick,
and just right.

She'd dreamed about Asher's cock, earlier in her home. That night by herself, she toyed with her clit. She'd hoped for him to be inside of her, begged for it in the silence of her bedroom. From then on, she'd painted his cock onto her mental canvas in long strokes with her imaginary paintbrush. But nothing had prepared her for the real thing.

And nothing would probably keep her from painting the reality in her head, in future nights to come. Nothing would change that, not even the sad fact that this man was a deranged killer.

That very fact shook her all the way down to the core.

I need professional help. Something is wrong with me. After I take down Asher, I'll get some help.

And then Asher's words stopped her mental tangent. "What are you thinking about?"

"Hmmm." She paused, rummaged for a quick thought, and blurted it out, "I'm wondering if Cupid is a sociopath or psychopath?"

A neutral mask slipped onto his face. "Interesting."

"What do you think?" she asked.

"I don't know."

"Surely, you would have an opinion," she pushed further.

"Surely." He sighed. "Is Cupid a sociopath or psychopath? That's a hard one. Why does it even matter?"

"In order to catch a killer, I have to get into the murderer's mind. In order to do that, I have to know something about his type of pathology. Some killers do it based on crimes of passion, those people tend to be narcissist and one-time murderers. They hate rejection. That isn't Cupid, he had no real relationship with his victim's women."

"Okay," he muttered.

"So we move on. Other killers are hit men commodifying

death, or gang members doing it for loyalty to the group. These aren't Cupid, either."

"I agree."

"Then we have the sociopaths and psychopaths."

Asher shifted uncomfortably in his seat.

"That's what I'm wondering." Diana placed her hands into her lap. "Which one is Cupid?"

"I don't know."

"But do you know anything about psychopaths and sociopaths?"

"A little. I read a few books."

"I know. I've seen your library. Most book worms would get an orgasm from just gazing at your bookshelves." She forced a fake giggle.

He didn't laugh, in fact, he didn't seem happy with this discussion at all.

I should stop, but I'm not. If he thinks I'm just going to sit around and be scared of him, without pushing his buttons and analyzing him, then he's wrong.

"But, what do you know about those types of murderers?" she asked. "Psychopaths and sociopaths."

Surprising Diana, Asher turned to her with a smirk that looked just as strained as her forced giggle. "A psychopath is mentally ill in some way. When he kills, it's usually someone he's known. In his mind, that person has provoked him into killing. I don't think that's Cupid at all. He's not crazy enough to think people are making him murder them. That would be just crazy. So is Cupid a sociopath?"

Asher's smirk widened into a wicked grin. "No. A sociopath is more hostile to society. At times, he murders with no real explanation and has no moral responsibility. I think Cupid possesses a moral duty to his world."

"But Cupid *is* hostile to society."

"I don't think so. Cupid may not be happy with a society that allows brothers to molest sisters and nothing gets done, or men to rape women and then have the court system slut-bash the victim until she is scared into dropping the case. Maybe, Cupid wants society to fix itself, and it's not. Instead, it drags around, polluting its citizens with celebrity gossip and drunken rants of stars. While ignoring the fat that there are children all over America sitting in broken homes. And they're scared, and there *are* real sociopaths, but those men are their fathers. And those men, spend their days battering the women they call their wives. And those men destroy every day of their kid's childhood until it's nothing but memories and nightmares of their mother's screams and her bloody nose. . ."

Diana's mouth dropped wide open.

"No, Diana, I don't think Cupid is a sociopath."

Diana twisted her fingers in her lap. "You don't think so because neither one of those definitions fit Cupid?"

He spat out the word, "Exactly."

"But Cupid is mentally ill. There's no denying that."

"No?" He looked at her.

"No. He's taking people's lives. Regardless of the reasoning, he's killing."

"Or is he saving other's lives? Is it not self-defense for others?"

"That's a stretch."

Rage thickened his tone and although Asher appeared calm, he was also stiff. "One of Cupid's *victims* molested his daughter. Do you think that she is unhappy with Cupid, now that her monster is dead?"

"Maybe."

"Maybe," he whispered. "And are you happy now that Neil is dead?"

Tension crept along her shoulders. That had not been the line of questioning that she'd wanted to pursue. She hoped to understand Asher some more, not have the topic turned back to her.

"Neil didn't truly hurt me," she replied.

"You're lying."

She let out an exasperated breath. "I wasn't defenseless. I could've left."

"When were you going to leave?"

"One day."

"When?"

The limo rounded a corner. A lovely home appeared with a white picket fence outlining it. Outside of the place, yellow police tape surrounded it and blocked all of the people standing outside. Tons of young girls stood there.

Diana checked her watch. "It's pretty late for these teens to be out tonight. Don't you think?"

"Maybe, they work here."

She raised her eyebrows and pointed to the house. "Here?"

"Yes, I've heard that this is a brothel that attends to dark needs."

"You've heard that, not been here yourself?"

He didn't answer.

So Asher killed in a brothel tonight? And he said it catered to dark needs?

The limo parked. Asher's driver jumped out, walked over to Diana's side, and opened the door. She got out, her legs barely able to hold her weight. She had to steady herself for a few seconds, push the limo conversation to the back of her head.

That was intense. I don't know how much more I can take. He's starting to undo me. I don't know if I want to run from him screaming, or high-five his hand for killing a molester and fuck his brains out.

Cool air bit at her skin. Police sirens and erratic chatter filled the air. More police officers walked up, but didn't come from any cars. The Ovid Island police department must've called over Miami-Dade to help them with this murder. Perfume laced the chilly breeze that pushed at her pony tail.

She took a step forward.

A huge van pulled up behind them. The Department of Children and Families stretched across the vehicle's side in thick block letters. Two women in law enforcement jackets guided several of the young girls to the van.

Young girls? Asher said the brothel dealt with dark needs.

Are the teen girls the dark needs? These guys were having sex with these young girls! God, men are disgusting.

She gritted her teeth.

Maybe, Asher should've killed all of the patrons tonight. It would have served those monsters right. Wait. What am I saying? People just can't go around killing people just because...they're hurting others.

Asher's voice came from behind. "Diana."

She turned and stiffened.

What the hell? How did he get behind me so fast? He's too silent, when he moves. Well...he's clearly had practice. Had he been in my apartment that night, when I thought someone was on my balcony?

She formed her fingers into fists, while embarrassment rained down on her.

He must've saw me masturbating to him. Did he? Why am I thinking about this now? What the hell is going on with me?

"Diana." He stood right behind her. Barely an inch existed between them. On his face, a haunting calm settled.

"Yes?" Her heart hammered in her chest. She tried to steady herself, but couldn't get a hold of her breathing.

"I decided not to walk in with you. I'm going to stay here." He glided his gaze along her body.

Everywhere he looked, her flesh tingled. "Why aren't you coming?"

His voice lowered as he spoke words that were sharp as a knife. "I'm not going to walk you in, because I've already seen this crime scene. Consider it my very own art installation. I went a bit over board with the knife, tonight. You found something tonight you weren't meant to. I didn't want you to find out like that. But..."

Their gazes met, and Diana was the only one who was close to looking away, and running. "Asher—"

He shook his head. "Pay no mind to the message in this crime scene, Diana. I needed you to feel the danger you were in so you would stay with me. If just for a few more days. I hadn't planned that our evening would go as it did. But now curiosity trapped the cat, and the cage...it is a big one, a whole island, and you're stuck here, my cat. Don't make me prove it." He leaned her way and landed a kiss onto her now shivering forehead. "This isn't to scare you. I just don't want you to do anything stupid, when you walk into the crime scene, witness the gore, and decide that one of those buffoons in uniforms will help you, I'll need you to rethink a foolish escape."

"A-asher—"

"No, you're not a cat. Curious, yes. But you're not a cat. You're a bird." He tilted to the side of his face and brushed his lips against her ear. "Ovid Island and my mansion is all your cage, and you are my bird. And like a lovely bird, I want to keep you all to myself. Do you have any questions?"

Her throat ran dry. Dread coated her veins. Shook through her core. Her stomach spun around like a washing machine's spin cycle. She wouldn't be eating anytime soon. She wanted to clutch her stomach, bend over, and vomit all over the ground.

"No, questions?" He whispered into her ear, and then leaned away, his lips brushed against her cheeks and delivered even more shivers, but were they fits of lust or fear, she had no idea.

He stepped back. "Some women would run, right now. They'd yell and scream out, 'This is the murderer. He's right here.' And what would happen? The police may or may not believer her, I may or may not be here once she's gotten enough people to stop focusing on the crime scene." He sucked his teeth a few times and shook his head. "To them, I'm not Cupid. I'm Asher Bishop, top contributor to Ovid Island police station as well as notable charity organizer in the state of Florida, much of my money going right to the Maimi-Dade police. I could hold my bloody bow and arrow in my hands, right now, and what would they do?"

Although her voice was rubbed raw, she mumbled, "Nothing."

"Nothing." He nodded. "They would do nothing."

He touched a stray hair on her face that had whipped out of her ponytail from the breeze. He glided his finger along that strand and then tucked it behind her hair. "And this is my beef with society. Money protects the rich and dominates the weak."

"I-I'm rich t-too."

"You've got money. You have prizes and awards."

"They'll believe me."

"They might or they might not. The odds aren't good for you, though."

"Then what is good for me right now?"

"Right now, you're someone I want to taste, to drown in, to love until my heart stops beating and my breath is nothing more than a dead man's gasp. Right now, I only want to protect Diana Carson. You have to believe that I never want to hurt you. Right now, you are my lover, and friend. But if you try to escape, if you point me out to the police as Cupid, I will no longer be your friend."

"I don't believe you."

"That's not a risk you want to take with me. My hand is skilled, when I hold my bow. It does not shake. My arrow hits the target. It will not waver."

She swallowed.

"Do you have any more questions?" he asked.

Nothing came out of her mouth.

Nothing moved within her.

Nothing else rushed to her head.

Nothing.

She was a sculpture of shock,
something chiseled from terror.

She could not move nor speak, think or even see the image of him in front of her.

It was all blurs and tears.

There were times in Diana's life, when she'd been scared. Like finding Gabby's maggot-infested corpse in her backyard or the first time Neil convinced her she was nothing more than his play-toy. But this? This moment shot up to the horizons as most fearful. All night, she'd romanticized Asher in her head, rationalized possibilities of why he was who he was.

Never did she consider the fact that,
regardless of his code,
regardless of him killing other monsters,
regardless of his appetite for her flesh,
taunting rhythm of his sex
and
the thickness of his cock
and
the undying passion that blazed in his eyes for her,
this man was still a murderer.
This man was dangerous,
And this man
would not let her go without having a final say,
and that statement could be deadly.

Asher wiped a tear away from her cheek and then glided his hand down further to her left breast.

Move my legs. Run. Open my mouth. Scream. Try to do something. Now.

"She loves me." He circled her hardening nipple. It puckered under her shirt. Her body battled her mind. Her flesh said lover. Her head said killer.

He moved his hand over to her right breasts and teased

the stiffening, and very hungry nipple. "She loves me not."

And she should of stepped away from him or screamed or ran or did anything a normal person would do when faced with an evil monster, but

A moan escaped her lips and she could do nothing more then drown in defeat.

"Are you scared, Diana?"

She was terrified. But she was also inexplicably intrigued, fascinated and completely taken aback with Asher Bishop. She knew she wouldn't run. The hunt wasn't over quite yet.

So instead of telling the truth, she whispered, "No, Cupid, I'm not."

VALENTINE PLAYLIST

Listen to the playlist on Spotify

Meg Myers – Desire

The Weeknd – Earned It

Sofia Karlberg – Crazy in Love

Ellie Goulding – Love Me Like You Do

Bebe Rexha – I'm Gonna Show You Crazy

Chelsea Lankes – Secret

Zack Hemsey – Vengeance

Broods – Sleep Baby Sleep

Melanie Martinez – Dead To Me

Iron & Wine – Such Great Heights

City and Colour – What Makes A Man

Eels – Love Of The Loveless

Gotye – Eyes Wide Open

Joshua Radin – Only You

Justin Nozuka – Save Him

Stars – Dead Hearts

KENYA WRIGHT

Writer. Lover. **Foodie.** Mother. **Book Addict.** Masturbator. **Comedian.** Super Hero. **Blogger.** Professional Adventurer.

ALSO BY KENYA WRIGHT

Series

Chasing Love (Interracial Erotic Romance)
An Arrangement of Love (Chasing Love #1)
A Test of Love (Chasing Love #2)

Bad for You (Interracial Dark Erotic Adventure Romance)
Bad for You 1: Sexual Deception
Bad for You 2: The Deadly Game
Bad for You 3: The Final Play
Bad for You Trilogy Boxed Set

Santeria Habitat Series (Dark Urban Fantasy/ Horror Romance)
Caged View (Book .5)
Fire Baptized (Book 1)
The Burning Bush (Book 2)

Wildfire Gospel (Book 3)

The Vampire King Series
Escape (Book 1)
Captured (Book 2)
Freed (Book 3)

Coventon Campus Series (Interracial Erotic Romance)
Complicated by You (Book 1)
Committed To You (Book 2)

Erotic Elf Series (Erotic Paranormal Romance)
Incubus Hunter (Book 1)

Billionaire Games Series (New Adult Erotic Romance)
Theirs to Play (Book 1)

Standalones

Chameleon

Flirting with Chaos
No Ordinary Love
The Babysitter (New Adult Erotic Short)
The Muse (Interracial Romantic Suspense)
Sexy as Sin (Interracial Erotic Romance)

JADE EBY

Once upon a time there was a little girl who fell in love with books then she grew up to write her own.

ALSO BY JADE EBY

Series

Back to Bad Series

Capricious (Book 1)

Voracious (Book 2)

Malicious (Book 3)

Audacious (Book 4)

Tenacious (Book 5)

Lacey: The Back to Bad Series Bundle

Whiskey and a Gun & The Finish Companions

Whiskey and a Gun

The Finish

Dirty Proof (Combined Whiskey and a Gun + The Finish + Bonus Material)

Standalones

The Right Kind of Wrong

Stuck: A Free Short Story for Newsletter Subscribers

Things We Never Say (not yet available for the public)

Made in the USA
Charleston, SC
04 June 2015